THE CAVER

Gothic Classics

THE CAVERN OF DEATH

EDITED BY ALLEN GROVE

VALANCOURT BOOKS
CHICAGO

Published by Valancourt Books
Chicago, Illinois

Originally published in 1794

First Valancourt Books edition August 2005

Cover design by Ryan Cagle
Introduction and notes © Allen Grove 2005
This edition copyright © Valancourt Books 2005
All Rights Reserved

The Cavern of Death
ISBN 0-9766048-3-3
Library of Congress Control Number: 2005924856

Printed in the United States of America

CONTENTS

Page

INTRODUCTION

Few living people have ever heard of the little book you hold in your hands. Even fewer have ever read it. But when *The Cavern of Death* first appeared in 1794, its anonymous author clearly succeeded in tapping the public's taste for all things Gothic. Between 1794 and 1801, the novel went through numerous English and American editions, and the work certainly sparked the imaginations of the Gothic writers who flooded the popular presses during the following two decades.

We know nothing of the anonymous author of *The Cavern of Death*. Was this work, like Matthew Lewis's *The Monk* (1796), written by a well-to-do gentleman for self amusement? Was the author, like Ann Radcliffe, a middle-class woman who wrote to fill up the tedious hours of a narrow domestic life? Or was it, like so many of the sensational works pouring out of Minerva Press, written by someone who could hardly afford paper and ink, but nevertheless recognized that the ever-growing popularity of Gothic fiction might just net a few pounds from a publisher? The novel gives us no answers to these questions.

Indeed, we would be hard-pressed to identify even the sex of the author. The work's sensational title, supernaturalism, Germanic setting, and violent denouement link it to what scholars often call "male Gothic." At the same time, the piece shares much with the writings of Clara Reeve and Ann Radcliffe, authors whose "female Gothic" moderates violence and presents a world that is ultimately more natural than supernatural. Moreover, these very categories of "male" and

1

"female" Gothic often fail to say much about the author, for works such as Mrs. Carver's *The Horrors of Oakendale Abbey* (1797) and Charlotte Dacre's *Zofloya: or, The Moor* (1806) reveal that women writers could be just a gruesome and sensational as the likes of Matthew Lewis. Similarly, George Moore, with his publication of *Grasville Abbey* (1793-1797) in *Lady's Magazine*, proved a male writer could be as proper and sentimental as a Radcliffe.

What is clear from *The Cavern of Death* is that the author borrowed from, among other works, both Horace Walpole's *The Castle of Otranto* (1765) and Clara Reeve's *The Old English Baron* (1778). From *Otranto* comes the novel's central prophecy, the ruler's panic over rights of succession, and the overheard dialogue between the heroine and her servant. From *Old English Baron* comes the hero's dream, the backdrop of the Crusades, and the final moral on the power of Providence and retribution. All three works center on questions of usurpation, the corruption of wealth and power, and the transformation of virtuous protagonists from lives of privation to affluence.

This is not to say that *The Cavern of Death* is an unoriginal plagiarism of earlier works. All early Gothic novels borrow from Horace Walpole and Clara Reeve in some way. The trappings of the genre—villainous patriarchs, haunted castles, mysterious screams, foreboding dreams, dark passageways—are precisely what make a work Gothic, so a degree of recycling is inevitable. Of course, deliberate plagiarisms certainly existed. One need only read *Father Innocent, Abbot of the Capuchins; or, The Crimes of the Cloister* (1802) to see an undisguised rip-off of Matthew Lewis's *The Monk* (1796). Yet *The Cavern of Death* would best be described as imitative, not entirely unoriginal. In fact, the anonymous author does add some creative new twists to the earlier stories: the servants Maurice and Elinor have more complex parts to play than the lower-class characters in earlier Gothics, and the typical Oedipal plot of sons overthrowing fathers, a plot that both Reeve and Walpole present implicitly, emerges in all its undisguised horror in *The Cavern of Death*.

The central Gothic stage piece to this work—the cavern itself—was certainly popular with Gothic novelists, even to the point of absurdity. Among the several thousand Gothic novels published in the late eighteenth and early nineteenth centuries, a remarkable percentage include at least one cave intertwined with their landscapes of cliffs, ravines, castles, abbeys, priories, ruins, and manor houses. In *Castle of Otranto*, the central hero protects the heroine in the recesses of a cave. Harriet Lee, in *Lothaire: A Legend* (1797), presents her protagonist stumbling across the remains of a murdered man within a cave, and both the plot and setting have striking parallels to *The Cavern of Death*. One need only take a brief survey of titles, as Montague Summers does in *The Gothic Quest*, to recognize the popularity of caverns to the genre: *The Romance of the Cavern* (1792), *The Haunted Cavern* (1796), *The Cavern of Strozzi* (1800), *St. Margaret's Cave* (1801), *The Cavern of Horrors* (1802), *The Lady of the Cave* (1802), *The Cave of Cosenza* (1803), *The Secret of the Cavern* (1805), *The Cave of St. Sidwell* (1807), *The Cave of Toledo* (1812), *The Cavern of Astolpho* (1818), and *The*

Hermit's Cave, or the Fugitive's Retreat (1821), to name only a few.

What exactly was the appeal of caves? On a basic level, they served to identify a work as Gothic and thus connect it to the genre's lucrative publishing market. As numerous literary scholars continue to struggle to define exactly what the term "Gothic" means, Eve Kosofsky Sedgwick's words help ground us in the obvious: "you know that a novel is of the Gothic kind... from the title." The author of *The Cavern of Death* clearly had this idea in mind, for the cavern actually plays a rather superficial role in the story. The cave's most important function was to get the curious reader to recognize the work as Gothic and grab it from the bookshelf at the local circulating library.

At the same time, cavernous settings were well suited to the aesthetic tastes of the Romantic period. In *A Philosophical Enquiry into the Origin of our Ideas of the Sublime and Beautiful* (1757), Edmund Burke theorizes that sublime, terror-provoking scenes can lead to seemingly paradoxical feelings of delight in an observer. Burke argues that threatening scenes of nature—rugged mountains, towering cliffs, stormy oceans, dizzying ravines, and, in this case, ominous caverns—call forth the most powerful and thrilling of our emotions, those connected with self-preservation. The pleasure such scenes can create in a reader was further explored by several Romantic period writers, including John Aikin in "On the Pleasure Derived from Objects of Terror" (1773) and Nathan Drake in "On Objects of Terror" (1798). Both essays delineate the fine line between pleasurable scenes of sublime terror and those scenes that are simply and irredeemably horrific.

Burke's *Enquiry* provides a laundry list of characteristics that make a scene sublime: lighting should be dark and gloomy; surfaces should be rugged and broken; colors should be black, brown, and deep purple; night should take precedence over day. Ann Radcliffe was most famous for employing Burke's theories within the pages of the Gothic novel. In *The Italian* (1797), for example, Ellena escapes the misery of her prison when she is able to look out of her turret upon "the wide and freely-sublime scene without." The landscape she views includes "vast precipices of granite," "rocky ledges," "lines of gigantic pine," and the thundering waters of a "dreadful pass." Ellena's emotion when viewing this scene comes straight from the pages of Burke and his imitators: she feels "dreadful pleasure." Although few Gothic writers quite match the rich and sublime landscapes of Radcliffe, the author of *The Cavern of Death* certainly toys with the same aesthetic concepts. The novel begins with the "gloomy scene" of a dark forest, and the eventual descriptions of the cavern present a space whose "bounds were lost in impenetrable darkness." Within these scenes both Sir Albert and his servant Maurice find their imaginations powerfully affected by the sublime.

Along with aesthetic principles of terror and the sublime, many Gothic novels such as *The Cavern of Death* are heavily anchored in the ideals of sensibility that feature so prominently in mid to late eighteenth-century British fiction. Such works tend to reveal the refined emotions, deep compassion, and sensitive tastes of their central protagonists. Ideal characters have a healthy balance of sense (rational thoughts stemming from the mind) and sensibility (feelings anchored in the heart). Sir Albert perfectly exemplifies this balance. Unlike his servant Maurice, Sir Albert uses reason to keep his imagination in check when confronted with terrifying or seemingly supernatural scenes. At the same time, he is not so rational as to entirely dismiss the possibility of supernatural events in the world around him. Also, the anonymous author goes to great length to illustrate Sir Albert's depth of feelings. From early in the novel, the hero displays his sensibility when he broods over his love for Constance and when he reveals himself to be a keen observer of her tears and blushes. Such character traits quickly distinguish Sir Albert from Frederic, a nobleman who exhibits "insensibility to the softer passions."

Constance's predicament, in fact, stems entirely from the lack of sensibility in the two men who control her future. Of her father, Constance notes that her "unwearied supplications repeatedly awakened his fiercest anger." She tells Elinor "how little he regards my tears." Likewise, when Constance appeals to the Baron to release her from their painful relationship, her plea entirely fails to move him. The novel thus exposes the shortcomings of a culture of sensibility. If legitimate contracts of marriage and property exchange are dependent upon the virtue, sympathy, and generosity of those in power, what happens when the powerful lack sensibility? *The Cavern of Death* and many other Gothic novels provide a simple answer: sensible characters, particularly women, quickly become the pawns and victims of tyrants. Admittedly, the level of social criticism in a sensational work such as *The Cavern of Death* is arguable, but the novel does suggest that if it were not for the rather implausible intervention of supernatural agents, the entire social and political system would be corrupt.

Furthermore, while we could easily dismiss *The Cavern of Death* as nothing more than sensationalized clap-trap set in a fantastic world far removed from reality, the original forum for the novel's publication complicates this idea. As the 1794 editor notes, the work made its first incomplete appearance in a daily newspaper, *The True Briton*. The serialization of a work in the 1790s was not uncommon (although the practice grew in popularity in the nineteenth century), but *The True Briton* certainly was an uncommon place to find a novel. From its first issues in 1793, the newspaper was not a publication that showed much interest in printing fiction. Nevertheless, there amongst reports of the French Revolution, transcripts of criminal trials, letters from George Washington, accounts of African exploration, and occasional advertisements for tonics that cure any and all ailments, we find the first installments of *The Cavern of Death*. And while the violence in France may have little to do with the violence in the novel, and while the warfare of twelfth-century crusaders may have little to do with eighteenth-century imperialism, the juxtapositions within the newspaper certainly beg us to make the comparisons.

Whatever the work's politics, *The Cavern of Death* is clearly the product of its cultural and historical contexts. The work may be set in the twelfth century, but the representations of marriage, property rights, sensibility, and the sublime all mark it as the distinct product of the late eighteenth century. And although the contemporary reader may still get swept up in the novel's plot, there are reasons why the work has been out of print for nearly two centuries. The exaggerated emotionalism and recycled Gothic devices that define the work understandably fell out of vogue in the mid-nineteenth century.

Yet we would be wrong to underrate the significance of *The Cavern of Death* within literary history. 1794 was just the beginning of the heyday of Gothic fiction, and we find many elements of this anonymous work reappearing in some of the most successful novels of the Romantic period, including the works of Ann Radcliffe and Matthew Lewis. The mistaken identities with the white plume look forward to Matthew Lewis's famous Bleeding Nun scene in *The Monk* (1796). When Sir Albert overhears Constance declaring her love for him, we are reminded of Vivaldi lurking in the garden outside of Ellena's window in Radcliffe's *The Italian* (1797).

Not only did other authors appropriate and recast scenes from *The Cavern of Death*, but the novel continued to reinvent itself in the early nineteenth century. Franz Potter notes that the work reappeared in chapbook form in 1802 as *The Black Forest; or the Cavern of Horrors! A Gothic Romance*, and again in 1830 as *The Black Forest; or, The Cavern of Death, A Bohemian Romance*. These latter reincarnations present the exact same story, but many scenes have been stripped of their sentimental trappings to leave us with little more than the most sensational elements of the plot.

The Valancourt Books edition of *The Cavern of Death* reproduces the book as it first appeared in 1794, using as its source the second edition London text published by J. Bell. No first edition of the novel is known to exist unless the original publishers considered the incomplete serialization of the work in *The True Briton* to be the first. I have preserved the original work's idiosyncrasies of punctuation, capitalization, syntax, and spelling. I have silently corrected just a few obvious errors, so the text here is nearly identical to that enjoyed by scores of readers over two hundred years ago. Much has changed during those two centuries, and for the contemporary reader the story is not just a journey to Germany's Black Forest in the twelfth century. It is also a journey back to the private chambers of eighteenth-century readers as they sat late into the night by the flickering light of a candle, losing themselves in a world of terror and death, but also a world where virtue was still rewarded and the heart could still triumph.

ALLEN GROVE
Alfred, NY, June 2005

ALLEN GROVE (Ph.D., University of Pennsylvania) is Associate Professor of English at Alfred University, where he teaches courses such as Tales of Terror, Gothic Fiction, and The Romantic Movement. His research and teaching often explore the interplay between sexuality, science, and genre in Gothic fiction. He is the editor of teaching editions of Ann Radcliffe's *The Italian* and Matthew Lewis's *The Monk* for College Publishing, and he is currently working on H. G. Wells's *The Invisible Man* for Broadview Press.

FURTHER READING

Aikin, John. "On the Pleasure Derived from Objects of Terror with Sir Bertrand, A Fragment." *Miscellaneous Pieces in Prose*. London: J. Johnson, 1773. (Reprinted in Radcliffe, Ann. *The Italian*. Ed. Allen Grove. Glen Allen, VA: College Publishing, 2005.)

Botting, Fred. *Gothic*. London: Routledge, 1996.

Burke, Edmund. *A Philosophical Enquiry into the Origin of our Ideas of the Sublime and Beautiful*. Notre Dame: University of Notre Dame Press, 1986.

Clery, E. J. *The Rise of Supernatural Fiction, 1762-1800*. Cambridge: Cambridge University Press, 1995.

Drake, Nathan. "On Objects of Terror and Montmorenci, A Fragment." *Literary Hours; or, Sketches Critical and Narrative*. London: J. Burkitt, 1798. (Reprinted in Radcliffe, Ann. *The Italian*. Ed. Allen Grove. Glen Allen, VA: College Publishing, 2005.)

Ellis, Kate Ferguson. *The Contested Castle: Gothic Novels and the Subversion of Domestic Ideology*. Urbana: University of Illinois Press, 1989.

Frank, Frederick S. *The First Gothics: A Critical Guide to the English Gothic Novel*. New York: Garland, 1987.

Lee, Harriet. "The Old Woman's Tale. Lothaire: A Legend." *Canterbury Tales for the Year 1797*. London: J. Robinson, 1797. (Reprinted in Radcliffe, Ann. *The Italian*. Ed. Allen Grove. Glen Allen, VA: College Publishing, 2005.)

Miles, Robert. *Gothic Writing 1750-1820: A Genealogy.* London: Routledge, 1993.

Potter, Franz, ed. *The Black Forest; or, The Cavern of Death. A Bohemian Romance.* 1830. Concord, NH: Zittaw Press, 2004.

Sedgwick, Eve Kosofsky. *The Coherence of Gothic Conventions.* New York: Methuen, 1986.

Summers, Montague. *The Gothic Quest: A History of the Gothic Novel.* New York: Russell & Russell, 1966.

Varma, Devendra P. *The Gothic Flame.* New York: Russell & Russell, 1966.

Williams, Ann. *Art of Darkness: A Poetics of Gothic.* Chicago: University of Chicago Press, 1995.

ADVERTISEMENT

THE little Tale which fills the following sheets, has, in part, already appeared in the Newspaper entitled THE TRUE BRITON. The interest which it excited, has induced the EDITOR of that Paper to offer it complete to the Public, the publication of the latter part of it in the Paper having been prevented by the constant succession of great and important events, which it was more peculiarly the business of a Newspaper to record.

If, in the detached and imperfect manner in which it appeared, curiosity was excited in no common degree, the EDITOR flatters himself that in its present form it will meet with the attention and approbation of the Public.

True Briton Office,
No. 5, *Catherine-Street, Strand,*
February 12, 1794

THE
CAVERN OF DEATH

"How awful is the approach of night amid these dreary shades!" cried the brave Sir Albert, as he traversed the most desolate part of the Black Forest. These were the first words that escaped his lips, since, about mid-day, he had entered that wild desart: and they were heard with satisfaction by Maurice, his Esquire and only attendant, whom respect had for some time with difficulty restrained from breaking the silence, which, interrupted only at intervals by the shrieks of the owl, or the flutter of the bat, seemed to deepen the horrors of that gloomy scene, and impressed on his mind a superstitious dread, which had no visible object, yet rose to the most agonizing height.

"Ah, Sir!" cried he, "what courage less intrepid than yours, would at this hour of darkness thus rashly penetrate the recesses of this Forest?"

"I have seen thee bold in battle, Maurice," said Sir Albert: "what mighty danger dost thou apprehend in this solitude, which thou canst deem it rashness in me to encounter?"

"Such scenes as these," returned the Esquire, "bring every deed of horror to one's thought: in

15

gloom like this, the Dæmons of the Air, and Spirits of the Dead, have power."

"My conscience is clear from every deed," said Sir Albert, "which should make me dread the vengeance of departed Spirits; and I trust that Heaven and good Angels will defend me from the malice of the Powers of Darkness. For any mortal foes I am armed, and fear not to encounter them."

"Would to Heaven I had turned my back," cried Maurice, "before I had reached this dismal place!"

"And how could we have avoided it?" demanded the Knight. "Thou hast thyself been my guide towards the Castle of Dornheim."

"I expected you would have reached it ere sunset, Sir," returned the Esquire: "but you have rode so slowly"—

"It is true," said Sir Albert: "my mind has been too much occupied with the thoughts of her on whose account, as to thee only I have confided, I have travelled hither, to leave me any leisure to recollect the tardy pace of my wearied horse."

He was then beginning to relapse into his former musing; but Maurice, who, in the sound of a human voice, had found some relief from the terrific phantasms which haunted his imagination, was eager to engage him in further discourse; and though already acquainted with the story of his love, yet, since he knew the satisfaction with which on that subject his master would always enlarge, he would not miss the opportunity of introducing it.

"Did you not tell me, Sir," said he, "that it was three years since last you saw the Lady Constance?"

"It is more," replied Sir Albert. "My heart would persuade me I had been separated from her during countless ages.—Ah! could I but know with what aspect she would review me!"

"It is impossible, Sir," said Maurice, "that to merit and constancy like yours she can be insensible."

"While I was at a distance from her," said Sir Albert, "I was pleased at being thus flattered; my own heart flattered me. I knew indeed, that for me she had never acknowledged any affection; but I knew that towards all others she had shewn the most marked indifference; and even from the solicitude with which she would often shun me, I could then draw a favourable inference, since, had she not been conscious that I adored her, she could have had no cause to treat me with less courtesy than others; and love so carefully concealed as mine, what but reciprocal love could have discovered? What other motive, have I vainly fancied, could have so frequently suffused her cheek with blushes, if I gazed on her, perhaps too eagerly? What else could have occasioned her emotion when we parted? Had I been indifferent to her, would she not—after so long an acquaintance with me, would she not have bidden me adieu? But the unfinished sentence died upon her lips; and, though she hasted from my presence, I had seen the tear that was starting from her eye."—Sir Albert paused, and was for some moments lost in the tender recollection; but presently recovering himself—"Such," said he, "have been the ideas which have enabled me to live, while I have been exiled from her presence; but, now that I approach her dwelling, now that my heart once more beats with the expectation to review her, I dare no longer cherish these flattering illusions. If I have deceived myself, how cruel will be my disappointment! And though my fondest hopes should have been just, should she have returned my tenderest affection, yet, after so long a separation, dare I believe that I still retain a place in her remembrance? May not some Lover, more worthy to possess her, have long ere this effaced every trace of me from her heart?"

"I have often wondered, Sir," said Maurice, "how, with so strong an attachment to the Lady Constance, you could resolve to quit Prague, where she resided, without declaring to her your sentiments, and endeavouring to obtain the avowal of hers."

"I have told thee, Maurice," returned Sir Albert, "that I had rather have died than have engaged her whose happiness I prized above my own, to share the fortunes of a man who had so little prospect of being able to place her in a rank worthy of her merit.—I do not now entertain any such presumptuous views: I wish but to see her: of what further I desire, my own heart is unconscious. Perhaps, since my Sword has purchased me some portion of renown; since I have received the honour of Knighthood from the imperial Frederick Barbarossa, and have acquired several noble friends who have promised me their services—perhaps, at some future period, I may find myself in a situation—But I have already said I will not indulge these thoughts. How far distant, Maurice, is the Castle of Hertzwald, where she now resides, from that of the Baron of Dornheim?"

"It is little more than a league," replied the Esquire. "I was frequently there while I dwelt at the Castle of Dornheim. It was then occupied by her Uncle; at whose death, a few months since, it devolved to her Father."

Another interval of silence now ensued; but Maurice, again solicitous to break it—"Did you never, Sir, acquaint Lord Frederic with your love?" said he.

"No, never," replied Sir Albert; "for though, from the time when it was my fortune to save his life in battle, he always professed for me the warmest friendship, yet his own insensibility to the softer passions, deterred me from placing in him the same confidence on that subject as I readily should on any other. It was by accident that he mentioned to me the arrival of the Father of Constance to settle so near the Castle of Dornheim, whither he had before so frequently invited me. Had he ever experienced a passion like mine, I have often since reflected, that the eager emotion with which I then accepted his invitation might sufficiently have discovered to him the secret of my soul."

"From his childhood," said Maurice, "Lord Frederic was ever of a haughty and violent temper—a stranger to tenderness and pity; and, though I had received from him many favours, and was yet more secure of the protection of the Baron his Father, I account myself fortunate in my removal from———But whence this sudden stream of light upon our paths?"

"Is it not the Moon emerging from behind a cloud?" said Sir Albert.

"The Moon is already set," returned the Esquire, trembling with renewed fears.

Sir Albert looked up—the thick interwoven branches of the trees in that spot obstructed his view; but, advancing a few paces to a more open place, he perceived a small black cloud, which seemed to hang lower than the rest, and hovered over his head with a tremulous motion, from the broken edges of which darted forth flashes of light, sufficiently strong to dissipate the darkness which by this time completely overspread the earth. Sir Albert gazed on it with wonder, and with that awe which any supernatural appearance necessarily impresses on the mind. The terrified Maurice dropped the reins, and in speechless agony expected some event of horror.—Presently they heard in the air a loud shriek, which seemed uttered by no mortal voice; and at the same moment the cloud burst asunder; and while the darker parts faded away, and mixed with the surrounding air, all the rays of light which had streamed from it, seemed to unite in one large ball of fire, and, descending towards the earth with a rapid course, sunk amid a thick cluster of trees, and still continued to gleam behind their branches. Sir Albert instantly spurred forward his horse, and hastened towards the spot. Maurice, with a trembling voice, urged him to forbear; but, regardless of his fears, the Knight advanced, and, forcing a passage through the trees, saw that the Meteor still appeared suspended over the entrance of a deep dark Cavern, which was illuminated by its splendour: but ere he could come quite up, it sunk into the abyss, and every object was enveloped in a thicker darkness than before.

Sir Albert, for some moments, hesitated how to act: his mighty courage, which always impelled him to attempt every perilous adventure, strongly urged him to enter the Cavern, and explore the mystery which some inward and inexplicable prepossession concurred with the appearance of the Meteor to persuade him he should discover within its recesses; yet the darkness of the night, which seemed to preclude the possibility of such a discovery, and the probability that the Cavern might be the abode of savage beasts or venomous serpents, to whose fury should he, in that dismal place, expose himself, he might perish ingloriously, the victim of an unjustifiable temerity, at last determined him to defer the attempt till the morrow, when he purposed to return with lights; and for the present to pursue his journey to the Castle of Dornheim, where he was already apprehensive he should arrive too late for admittance. On returning to Maurice, he found him so overcome with terror, that he seemed scarcely to retain his senses: he talked wildly of a Spirit who pursued him, and of voices issuing from the Cavern. Sir Albert, though seldom moved to anger by any trivial cause, was at last impatient of fears he deemed so groundless, and reproved his folly with a harshness which seemed in some degree to recall him to himself.

They had not proceeded far, before they discovered a light through the trees: Maurice started, and would have turned back; for the Meteor still haunted his imagination, and left him no recollection of the vicinity of the Castle of Dornheim, whence Sir Albert concluded the light to proceed, and he soon found that his conjecture was just. On approaching nearer, he perceived that the whole front of the Castle was illuminated; and, amid many voices which he heard within its walls, he could distinguish the strains of mirthful music. Though the soul of Sir Albert was little disposed to share in this apparent festivity, he was pleased to find that the drawbridge was not yet raised, nor the porter retired to rest; which had he found to be the case, it had been his intention rather to take up his lodging for that night in the Forest, than to disturb the family at an unseasonable hour. On sounding a horn which was suspended by the gate, it was instantly unbarred, and a Seneschal came forth, and invited him to enter, telling him, that on that day admittance was free to all. Sir Albert could not but demand what prosperous event was the occasion of the rejoicing which he perceived in the Castle. The Seneschal replied, that it was to celebrate the approaching nuptials of the Baron with a Lady whom he had for some time courted, and which, it had been that morning settled, should take place in three days time. The Knight then demanded to speak with Lord Frederic: he was conducted into a spacious apart-

ment, where he had not waited long before Lord
Frederic came.

Sir Albert, having raised the vizor of his casque,
advanced to accost him; but he no sooner recognized
the Knight, than, not allowing him time to speak, he
embraced him with an eagerness sufficiently expressive of his joy. "Is it possible, my friend!" cried he,
"that I behold thee here? Thy arrival at this juncture
was the object of my most ardent wishes; it was an
happiness to which my hope durst scarce aspire."

"I consider so kind a welcome, my Lord!" replied
Sir Albert, "as an additional proof of your friendship
towards me; and it enhances the pleasure this meeting has afforded me."

"Ascribe not my joy to friendship only," replied
Lord Frederic: "my own interest has too principal a
share in it.—To see thee at any time I should rejoice;
but now, when to valour like thine I may owe the
felicity of my life, thy fortunate arrival has recalled
me from desperation."

"What mean you, my Lord?" said the Knight;
"what cause can have reduced you to despair? and in
what manner can I be so happy as to serve you?"

"It is not now a season to explain myself more
fully," said Lord Frederic: "among the crowds who
enter promiscuously every apartment in the Castle, I
know not who may over hear me. To-morrow morning we will walk together in the Forest. Mean-while
I will lead thee to the feast: after thy journey hither,
refreshment may be welcome to thee; but, amid the
sports and folly of my Father's servile train, let the

recollection of our mutual amity possess thy mind; and let me find thee to-morrow, as thou hast ever hitherto appeared to me, a friend on whom I may rely."

The words of Lord Frederic, and still more, the agitation of his manner, surprized and alarmed Sir Albert: he renewed his assurances of his readiness to serve him, and they walked together to the Great Hall of the Castle. Lord Frederic there presented his newly arrived friend to his Father, who was encircled by a crowd of the guests who were come to partake of his festival. The Baron, on hearing his name announced, turned hastily round; but, instead of bidding him welcome, he for some moments regarded him, and continued silent.

Sir Albert, who had expected a different reception, was in some degree confused at this; and Lord Frederic, visibly offended at his Father's coldness towards a friend to whom he owed so much—"I thought, my Lord," said he, "I had already informed you, that it was this valiant Cavalier who exposed his own life to the most imminent danger, to rescue me from the enemies against whom, wearied, and fainting with loss of blood, I was no longer able to defend myself."

"And I will eagerly embrace every opportunity, my Son!" returned the Baron, starting as if from a deep musing, "to prove to him and to the world, how dearly I prize that life which he then preserved.— Most valiant Sir!" continued he, addressing himself to Sir Albert, "I must entreat your forgiveness, if, at the moment of your approach, my thoughts were so far engrossed by other matters, that I did not, immediately on the mention of your name, recollect the vast obligation I was under to you. It is with unfeigned joy that I embrace the deliverer of my Son, and personally express to him the gratitude and esteem which I long have borne him. You are most welcome to my Castle; and I flatter myself that you will shew, by the length of your abode in it, your persuasion of the satisfaction your presence affords me."

Sir Albert made a suitable reply to this compliment; and, after a few more expressions of courtesy, the Baron entreated him to disarm. The Knight at first refused; but on being further pressed, he complied; and retiring to a private chamber, he was attended by his own Esquire, and by one of the domestics of the Castle, who, by the Baron's command, brought him a rich robe to put on, after he should have quitted his arms.

As Maurice was unbuckling his corslet, Sir Albert perceived that his hand trembled—"Thou hast not yet," said he, "recovered from the terror which seized thee in the Forest."

The Esquire acknowledged that he had not.

"Did you meet with any alarming adventure there, Sir?" said the Baron's domestic.

"We passed near the mouth of a Cavern," returned Sir Albert: "what terrific visions Maurice might behold there, himself can best inform you."

"The mouth of a Cavern?" exclaimed the domestic; "and near this Castle?"

"Scarce a furlong distant," replied the Knight.

"And did you then see nothing there, Sir?" rejoined the other.

"What should you suppose me to have seen?" demanded Sir Albert, with some emotion.

"So many sights of terror have been seen in that spot," returned the domestic, "that it is long since any of us have dared to approach it. That Cavern is assuredly the habitation of the Infernal Spirits. Sometimes there have been heard in it hollow groans, or shrieks of anguish; sometimes, noises resembling the rushing of torrents, or the rumbling of pent-up vapours. There is a report, that some murder was formerly perpetrated there, and that it is the avenging Spirit of the Dead who still haunts the place where he was disunited from his body."

"Were these opinions current, Maurice," said Sir Albert, "during the time of thy abode at this Castle?"

"I have heard some mention of them, Sir," returned the Esquire, paler than before.

"And how long is it since these strange noises and appearances were first noticed in the Cavern?" said the Knight.

"I have been told, Sir," returned the Baron's domestic, "that the first portentous circumstance observed there, was a light which shone round the mouth of it, some four or five and twenty years ago, nearly about the time when the Castle came into the possession of the present Lord. But I can aver nothing on the subject with any certainty, as it is scarcely three months since I came hither myself; and all the events of that distant period have been variously related to me by different persons belonging to the Castle."

"Thou, Maurice, camest hither with the present Baron," said Sir Albert—"Dost not thou remember any further particulars? Did no tradition point out who this murdered person was supposed to have been?"

"Some Traveller, wandering in the Forest, Sir," replied Maurice: "but indeed the murder was only a vague report; and the Cavern had been dreaded equally by the neighbouring people, from a period far earlier than that of the accession of the Baron."

"Has this Cave any particular name?" demanded the Knight.

"It is called the *Cavern of Death,*'" returned the domestic.

Sir Albert made an end of attiring himself in silence; for this account of a place where he had himself witnessed a circumstance which he believed to be supernatural, had made a deep impression on his mind.—His desire to penetrate the innermost recesses of the Cavern was now stronger than ever: he judged it, however, expedient to forbear mentioning the design he had conceived, since he knew not who might have an interest in preventing the dire discoveries to which he was inwardly persuaded it would lead.

---

* *Die Hole des Todes*, is the name which it still retains; and the neighbouring Peasantry at this day dread to approach it, and entertain many wild and superstitious ideas respecting it.

27

As soon as he was ready, he returned to the Great Hall, where the Baron and his Son received him with new demonstrations of joy. A magnificent banquet was now spread. The Baron placed Sir Albert in the most honourable seat, nearest himself, and treated him as a guest of the highest distinction. Sir Albert, however, could not but observe, that from time to time he fixed his eyes on him with a remarkable intentness, but they were instantly averted if his encountered them. For Lord Frederic, his stern and frowning brow sufficiently expressed the disturbance of his mind: he joined in no discourse with any of the guests; and if ever a momentary smile dispelled the gloom of his countenance, it was when he looked towards his newly arrived friend. As Sir Albert extended his hand across the table, the lustre of a ring he wore on his finger caught the Baron's eye. He praised its richness, and requested permission to view it more closely. Sir Albert immediately took it off, and presented it to him. It was a large ruby, encircled with brilliants. The Baron examined it with great attention, and declared the ruby to be the most valuable he had ever seen.

"I am myself, Sir Knight," added he, "well skilled in jewels; and you have shewn yourself to be equally so, by the purchase of so fine a stone."

"I assure you, my Lord," returned Sir Albert, "I am totally unqualified to judge of its value: it bears, indeed, an high one to me—not on account of its own richness, but because it is the only relic I retain of my deceased Father."

The Baron again praised the beauty of the ring, and returned it to its owner.

The banquet was not ended till a very late hour. At last, when it was almost morning, the guests departed, well satisfied with the hospitality they had experienced; and the Baron himself conducted Sir Albert to the chamber he had caused to be prepared for him, where, after many expressions of courtesy, he left him. In his way thence he met Maurice, who was going to attend upon his master. He immediately knew him, and expressed his satisfaction at his return to the Castle.

"I was sorry," added he, "that you should receive any cause for displeasure in the service of my Son; but though you chose to quit him, you may remain assured of my friendship and protection."

The Esquire thanked him for this assurance; and the Baron, telling him he would gladly speak further with him, desired him to repair to his apartment in the morning, as early as he should rise.

Maurice then attended his master, who soon dismissed him, and retired to rest; but it was long before sleep closed his eyes. Lord Frederic's mysterious expressions, and visible melancholy, rendered him anxious for further discourse with him; but he was yet more impatient to enter the Cavern, of which such strange accounts had been given him. He lost himself in vain conjectures respecting the cause of the noises and extraordinary appearances reported to proceed from it, and was persuaded that some deed of horror had been perpetrated there; though, had it not been for what he had himself observed, he might probably have treated the whole as the vision of the idle superstition of the peasants. At last his thoughts, seldom so long diverted from the object of his dearest affections, returned into their usual channel: the idea of his vicinity to the dwelling of the Lady Constance possessed itself of his soul, and left him no recollection of any thing beside. His imagination seemed already to have exhausted every possible circumstance which might attend their meeting; yet he continued retracing each fond idea, till, overcome by weariness and watching, he at last fell into a slumber.

His dreams did not correspond with the latest subject of his meditations: they were dismal, mysterious, and terrific.—He imagined himself again seated at the Baron's festive board; the strains of music again sounded in his ears; mirth sparkled in the eyes of every guest, and the light of innumerable tourches diffused an artificial day: when suddenly their brightness was eclipsed by the interposition of a dark shadow, which skimmed along the table, and sometimes seemed to rest hovering over the centre of it. Sir Albert and all the guests looked up, and beheld a most hideous Spectre, of a gigantic size, traversing the air above their heads with a slow and melancholy flight; his stern and threatening aspect appalled every heart. As they regarded him, an hollow voice proclaimed,

    —"The fated hour is come!
And the fell powers of Vengeance are abroad!"

The Castle shook from its foundations: the Spectre waved his wings, and immediately a thick mist arose, which in a few moments enveloped all who were present. Sir Albert could no longer distinguish any object; but, amid the general darkness, his ears were thrice assailed with skrieks of horror. On a sudden, a vivid ray of light streamed from the East upon the spot on which he stood; he turned his eyes, and beheld a cloud resembling that which the preceding evening had directed his steps to the *Cavern of Death;* and by degrees he discerned, seated in the midst, a Warrior, clad in refulgent arms, and bearing on his breast the ensign of the Cross. The radiance which surrounded him dispersed the mist; and Sir Albert found, that of all the company who had been assembled at the feast, himself alone remained. The horrible Spectre had also disappeared at the approach of this less terrific phantom, who, descending from the cloud, and regarding Sir Albert with a look of celestial benignity, extended his arms to embrace him. Sir Albert, with an emotion which he had never before experienced, hastened towards him; but no sooner did the Phantom meet his touch, than its substance seemed to fade away; its shining arms dropped off, and the Knight perceived that he had folded a skeleton to his breast.—He started, and unclosed his arms with horror! yet it fell not to the ground; but, waving in the air a bloody sword, which at first it had not wielded, it distinctly uttered, in a thin faint voice, these words:

"From this cold hand thou must receive this sword,
Ere I can be aveng'd, or thou restor'd!"

And immediately vanished.

The horror it had inspired awoke Sir Albert. A dewy chill had invaded his limbs;—for some moments he scarce durst raise his eyes, lest they should meet some shape of terror; and the fear which now possessed his soul, was perhaps the more painful to him, because it was the first time he had ever experienced its power. By degrees, he became sensible that it had no other object than a dream; but, though he then soon shook it off, yet still the impression continued which that dream had made on his mind; and he was persuaded that it was some vision of mysterious import, and not any common creation of fancy, which had thus deeply moved him.—The morning was now far advanced. Sir Albert rose, seated himself by the window, and mused. The words of the Apparition, who had so suddenly assumed a form so ghastly, still rebounded in his ears; and he felt a strong conviction that some event of futurity would unfold to him their oracular meaning. He was unable to guess who the person should be whose Spirit thus seemed to call for vengeance; yet he was sometimes inclined to suppose it might be the same whom popular report averred to have been murdered in the *Cavern of Death.*

His thoughts were still wholly occupied by conjectures on this subject, when a message was brought to him from the Baron, inviting him to breakfast with him in his apartment. He complied, and found the Baron alone, and was received by him with the warmest expressions which courtesy could dictate. The compliments he paid to his character, and former heroic actions, were indeed such as gave pain rather than pleasure to Sir Albert, whose modesty was such as rendered all praises of himself extremely irksome to him. He therefore availed himself of the earliest opportunity to turn the discourse on other subjects, and readily answered such questions as the Baron put to him, relative to the countries he had visited in his travels. He asked him, at last, of what place he was a native?

"I was born in the City of Prague, my Lord," returned the Knight.

"Was your Father, then, a Bohemian?" demanded the Baron.

"It may seem strange, my Lord," replied Sir Albert, "to say, that I know not with any certainty what was my Father's country: my Mother, Isabella Von Glatzdorff, was one of the most ancient families in Bohemia; but I lost both my Parents too early to retain any recollection of them: I am only acquainted with their misfortunes, and my own share in them, from the report of an Uncle, to whom I owed my education."

"Your words excite my curiosity," said the Baron: "may I enquire what those misfortunes were, in which you were so early involved?"

"I can relate the story but imperfectly, My Lord," returned the Knight. "My Uncle, in his youth, assumed the Cross, and engaged in the service of Baldwin the Second of Jerusalem, at that time much straitened by his enemies; and in the battle in which that Prince was unfortunately taken prisoner by the Turkish Emir Balac, he was generally reported to have been slain; but fate had reserved him for severer sufferings: he also had fallen alive into the power of the Infidels, among whom he remained in a rigorous captivity during eleven years. At last he contrived means to escape; but on his return to Prague, when he expected to have been received with joy by his family, he experienced the most cruel disappointment. His Parents, and his elder Brother, were dead: the latter, believing him no more, had bequeathed all his estates to a distant relation, omitting to make any reservation in his favour, in the event of his return. His sister alone survived; but it was many days before he could discover the miserable place of her abode; and, when his search was at last successful, what were the feelings of his generous heart, when he found her bereft of reason, and supported by the charity of strangers? From them he learned, that, after the death of her Parents, she had disobliged the Brother on whom she was left dependent, by her marriage with Rodolph Von Fahrenbach, a young stranger, of whom they could give no further account than that he had distinguished his valour in a contest with a Bohemian Nobleman, who also courted her favour; and that, shortly after their marriage, he had quitted her, to engage in a crusade, in compliance with a vow he had made previous to his acquaintance with her: that he had been absent two years; at the end of which time certain intelligence of his death was brought to her; the shock proved greater than she was able to support; it threw her into a delirious fever, from which, for many days, the utmost danger was apprehended; her life was however preserved, but her senses never returned to her. She had been for some months in this deplorable situation, when she was visited by her Brother, who immediately took her, and me (who had not been born till after my Father's departure) to his own house, when he employed every means for her recovery which the advice of the ablest physicians could suggest; but his cares were unavailing; the deep melancholy which continually preyed upon her mind, soon threw her into a decline; and within a year after his return, she died, the unhappy victim of despair. From that time, all the affection which my Uncle had borne her, seemed transferred to me. He made many inquiries after my Father's family, wishing to obtain their protection for me; but he could not discover in what part of Germany they were settled. My Mother, in a moment of phrenzy, had destroyed all the letters she had received from my Father, and indeed every memorial of him, except this ring, which you, my Lord, last night observed: it had been his first gift to her; and, till the latest moment of her life, she would never suffer it to be taken from her finger. But, if my Uncle failed in discovering my other relations, he never permitted me to feel their loss. His income was small; but he abridged his own expences, that he might be enabled to defray those of my education; and, as soon as I was at an age to bear arms, he led me himself into the paths of glory. Unacquainted with my real Father, I always venerated this generous kinsman as such: he has now been dead some years; but I shall ever respect and love his memory, and the sense of the gratitude I owe him will remain with me to the last hour of my existence."

The Baron heard this narrative with much attention; and the various changes of his countenance expressed how deeply he interested himself in the misfortunes of the unhappy Isabella. Sir Albert observed his concern, and felt himself under an obligation to him for it. They continued in discourse for some time longer; when the Knight, recollecting the desire Lord Frederic had expressed to see him, thought it time to go in quest of him: he rose, and bade the Baron adieu for the present; and with mutual courtesy they parted.

In a long gallery which he passed through in his way from the Baron's apartment, he found Lord Frederic, walking to and fro with hasty steps.

"What interesting discourses can have detained you so long with my Father?" said that impetuous youth: "I have been here almost an hour, waiting till you should quit him."

"I staid the longer with him," replied Sir Albert, "because I expected you would meet me in his apartment: as you came not thither, I concluded you were otherwise engaged. I was now about to seek you; but

I did not imagine I should find you here awaiting me."

"I could not just now appear before my Father," said Lord Frederic: "my mind is too much agitated to allow me to dissemble. But this is not a place for private conference; let us go where we may discourse without danger of being overheard."—And, as he spoke, he took the arm of Sir Albert, and led him out of the gallery.

They passed onwards to the Castle Gate: Lord Frederic threw it open, and went forth into the Forest.—Sir Albert still accompanied him; and neither broke silence till they reached a deep glade, entirely excluded from all view of the Castle. Here they stopped—Lord Frederic quitted Sir Albert's arm, and regarding him earnestly, "I would know," said he, "whether I might indeed accost thee by the title of my friend?"

"Can you think so meanly of me, my Lord," returned the Knight, "as to suppose I should ever afford him for whom I had professed a regard, any cause to question its sincerity? I shall certainly never be unmindful of the many courtesies I have received from you; and I trust I may appeal to more than words, to prove the reality of the friendship I have borne you."

"It is true, dear Albert!" cried Lord Frederic; "I have not forgotten that to thy friendship I have owed my life, while mine towards thee has hitherto had no opportunities of shewing itself but in words and vain professions: hereafter, I trust, I may be able to give thee more solid proofs of gratitude. But first, I must again have recourse to the valour to which I am already so much indebted, for a service, which, if it refuse to render me, it were better it had never been exerted in my cause.—Life is only a blessing to the happy!"

"And what unexpected calamity, my Lord," said Sir Albert, "can have rendered you otherwise? Your perturbed looks, and many expressions which have fallen from you, lead me to apprehend some dreadful evil."

"But for thee," said Lord Frederic, "and I must endure the greatest; I must endure the greatest; I must behold the Mistress whom I love to distraction, in another's arms."

"And have you then felt the power of love, my Lord?" cried the Knight;—"but who is your fair Mistress? and how can I preserve her to you?"

"Before I disclose further, Sir Albert," said the youth, "you must solemnly promise me that you will assist my views."

"It were unnecessary to bind myself by any promise," returned he, "since, without that additional tie, I shall undoubtedly act on this, and on every future occasion, as friendship and the laws of honour shall require of me."

Lord Frederic pressed him further; but Sir Albert liked it not. His intimacy with that young Nobleman had arisen, not from any similarity of sentiment or of temper, but solely from their having been companions in war; and it had assumed the name of friendship, since Lord Frederic, preserved by Sir Albert

from the most imminent danger, and therefore con-
sidering him as the bravest of men, had eagerly
courted his society, and had, on every occasion, professed for him the highest regard. But, though his
unremitted courtesies had gained him a considerable
share of the affection of Sir Albert, they had not so
far blinded his judgment, as to induce him to concur
implicitly, and without further information, in the
projects of a youth, whose impetuous passions, but for
his own more prudent counsels, would, he knew, on
many former occasions, have involved him in the
greatest indiscretions. When Lord Frederic found
that he persisted in his refusal to engage himself by
the promises he required, he at last ceased to insist on
it, and, telling him that he would evince to him how
great a dependence he placed on his friendship, he
proceeded to relate the circumstances which had induced him to demand his aid.

"Thou may'st remember," said he, "that I was sent
for by my Father from the Camp, in a manner which
led me to conclude that he had some motive of importance for requiring my return.—I came hither by
hasty journeys; and, on my arrival, was informed of
his intended marriage, which I found he was desirous
of communicating to me in person, lest, hearing it
from others, I might be induced to suppose my own
interests endangered, and to attempt some opposition
to his designs. I was the less surprized at this intelligence, because I knew, that, since the death of his
other Sons, it had been a constant subject of uneasi-
ness to him to behold in me the last of his race: I have

heard that he suffered himself to be alarmed by some prophecy or dream, I know not particularly what, which had denounced some dreadful fate to his family, whenever one male should be the only survivor of it. He never clearly explained himself to me on this point; but he had often pressed my marriage with a degree of earnestness which was very irksome to me, and had always appeared displeased at the invincible reluctance I had discovered. When, therefore, he acquainted me with his wish to present me to the Lady to whom he expected me to pay the duties of a Son, I attended him to her abode, not without some satisfaction that he had rather chosen to offer her his own hand, than to attempt to compel me to give her mine. But how can I express to you, Sir Albert! the sudden change which the sight of this peerless beauty effected in my heart? That heart hitherto so insensible, in a moment confessed the power of her irresistible charms. I had been too little interested in her to make any previous inquiries respecting her; I had not even been told she was fair:—judge, therefore—if ever your temper, softer than my own, has felt the influence of beauty—judge what were my emotions, when in her to whom I was introduced as to my future Step-mother, I beheld the most lovely creature that the world certainly ever saw! With the idea of my Father's Wife, I had connected that of proportionable age; but her's appeared not to exceed my own. Her form—her eyes—I cannot describe them, Sir Albert!—If my hopes in you deceive me not, I trust you will ere long behold her; and believe me, I do not mean to under-rate your services, when I tell you that the sight of such charms were alone a recompense worthy of them. The only embellishment of which her beauty was capable, it received when I was presented to her; she was desired to consider me as the Son of him to whom her hand was destined: she sighed as she regarded me; and her cheek, before almost colourless, was suffused with a blush, as she permitted me to take her hand, which, with an eagerness which banished from my remembrance every idea of the character in which the salute was permitted me, I pressed to my enraptured lips. She sighed more deeply than before, and drew her hand suddenly from me; her eyes filled with tears, and she turned away.—I do not surely flatter myself, Sir Albert, when I impute these marks of sorrow to the impulse of sentiments with which my appearance had inspired her: she regretted that it was to my Father, and not to myself, that she was promised; and it was her apprehension lest this emotion should be remarked by those in whose eyes it would be deemed a crime, which made her so hastily quit a situation in which, if I may judge from my own feelings, she would have found it so difficult to dissemble hers. It was probably fortunate for me that her discretion, or perhaps her timidity, exceeded mine: I should questionless have otherwise betrayed to her Father and my own, the new-born passion, which, as soon as I had recovered from that kind of trance into which the first view of her charms had thrown me, every motive so strongly urged me to conceal. Yet I think some infatuation, rather than my dissimulation, must have so far blinded their eyes as to prevent their discovering it—I have reason to be persuaded it has entirely escaped their observation. The deep melancholy to which I have resigned myself, has indeed attracted my Father's notice; but he ascribes it to my apprehensions lest my interest should be endangered by this projected alliance. Nor indeed, were my mind free from other cares, would it perhaps be easy on that head; for, were he to have other sons, it were by no means improbable but that so young and beautiful a wife might have sufficient influence over him, to induce him to make such dispositions in their favour as would materially diminish the inheritance I have long been taught to expect. But such considerations are too mean to engage at present my attention.—To attain the possession of this incomparable Fair, I would joyfully resign any riches, any honours; but the thought of beholding her in the arms of another, of seeing her sacrificed to one whose age and grey hairs ought to have forbidden him to aspire to the possession of so lovely a maid—Sir Albert! it drives me to distraction! madness will seize my brain, if thou deny me thy compassion.—Dost thou hesitate? Canst thou refuse to succour me?"

"I must sincerely compassionate you, my Lord!" returned the Knight; "and I must grieve that you have resigned your soul to a passion which involves you in so many difficulties."

"It involves me in no difficulties," cried Lord Frederic eagerly, "from which thou canst not extricate me."

"Is it in any plan for carrying off this Lady," said Sir Albert, "that you require my assistance? Let me entreat you, my Lord, to consider coolly the peculiar circumstances in which—"

"I have considered," interrupted Lord Frederic; "and I know that there is but one possible means by which, without ruining my fortune, I can attain the secure possession of my Love.—It is to the Baron of Dornheim that her hand is promised by her ambitious parent.—Could it be possible for me to elude his vigilance, and to steal her from his Castle, I might be well assured that the estates of my incensed Father never would be mine; but were that title, were those estates now mine—Sir Albert! canst thou term thyself my friend, and not recollect that thy hand might render them such?"

Sir Albert started! he regarded Lord Frederic with a look of surprize and apprehension, and read on his gloomy brow the confirmation of the fears his words had suggested.

"I would myself be Baron of Dornheim," said Lord Frederic, after a pause: "Dost thou not understand me?"

"I dare not imagine I do," replied the Knight, turning from him with horror.

"Hadst thou ever loved, Sir Albert!" resumed Lord Frederic, "thou wouldst have felt, that to know in any man a rival, suffices to obliterate from the mind every former sentiment with which he may have been regarded.—I see thou hast understood me; that thou knowest I wish my rival removed, and that thou art shocked at the idea of the relationship he bears me:— but he is not thy Father!—I mean not to lift my own arm against him; but thou—thou, who art my friend, and who art bound to him by no tie of kindred or of duty—when thou considerest that the whole future happiness of my life depends on this short anticipation of the fate which his years announce cannot be far distant—"

"What have you ever observed in my character, my Lord," said Sir Albert, looking sternly round, "which can authorize you to offer me this insult? Am I an assassin?"

"Do not suppose me capable of insulting you, my friend!" returned Lord Frederic; "I know your high sense of honour; and trust me, I would employ your valour in no enterprise unworthy of it. Could the Baron be surprized at any disadvantage, I should never have had recourse to your arm; among my own followers I could have found those who would faithfully have executed my purpose.—But that were impossible—he never, even for a moment, is alone. I know not what is his motive; I have not heard that he has any enemy of whose designs he is apprehensive; yet his conduct is such as might induce such a supposition. Throughout the day, some of his attendants are always with him; and at night, a priest and two domestics constantly sleep in his chamber. This circumstance, as you will perceive, must render vain every hope of surprizing him; and, if he has leisure to defend himself, your prowess only were a match for his. In his youth, you may have heard, he was a Warrior of the first renown; nor has age yet unnerved his arm. I know you would scorn to contend with an enemy of inferior might; but be assured, my friend—"

"Call me no longer such!" cried Sir Albert; "I disclaim the friendship of a parricide!"

Lord Frederic was provoked at the reproach; but, having already so far put himself in Sir Albert's power, he durst not express his indignation, but rather sought, by new entreaties, to bend him to his purpose. "Were my love less ardent," said he, "my schemes would be less desperate; but who, under the dominion of so irresistible a passion, could forbear the only means of attaining that felicity, which otherwise, within three short days, must be for ever placed beyond his reach? If I loved a meaner beauty, it might perhaps be possible I should resign her; but who that adored the Lady Constance—"

"Constance!" exclaimed Sir Albert, starting wildly; "is it Constance?"

"Constance of Hertzwald, is the Lady destined to my Father's arms," returned Lord Frederic, "if thou refuse, in pity to her and to thy friend, to rescue her youthful charms from such a sacrifice, and to give her to a Lover more worthy to enjoy them!"

"And does the Lady Constance return thy love?" said Sir Albert, trembling, and scarcely able to pronounce the question.

"I cannot doubt it," replied Lord Frederic: "I have never indeed received from her lips the transporting assurance, since I have never been able to obtain an interview with her but in my Father's presence; but one of her women, who is my only confident, assures me that she is very averse to the marriage proposed, and that many circumstances have rendered it very evident that she secretly loves another. That I was the man so blest, I durst not positively assure myself till the last time I visited her Father's Castle; but then, her looks, her whole demeanour, were such as it were impossible to misinterpret. She seemed unable to avert her eyes from my person; yet if I, or any other, appeared to notice the earnestness with which she regarded me, she was covered with confusion; and many times a sigh escaped her, which still more strongly spoke the tender sentiments which occupied her soul."

While Lord Frederic was thus speaking, the countenance of Sir Albert was flushed with a thousand conflicting passions. Twice he laid his hand upon his sword; and twice, even amid the transports of jealous fury, he recollected that he was the guest of him on whom he would have drawn it; that he was himself armed, and that his rival was not—he recollected, and he was master of the emotion.

"We may meet again, Lord Frederic!" cried he— "if we do, remember that we meet no more as friends!" And, as he spoke, he turned from him, and walked with hasty strides towards the thickest shades of the Forest.

Lord Frederic, astonished at his demeanour, for which, ignorant that he had ever seen the Lady Constance, he could assign no adequate cause, stood for a moment surprized. He would then have called him back; but Sir Albert only quickened his pace.—Fired with rage, he would then have followed him, to demand an explanation of his words, and still more of the menacing air with which they had been uttered; but he was now lost among the trees, and Lord Frederic sought him in vain.

Sir Albert, mean-time, careless whither he went, walked on. He had fancied his own passion hopeless; but, at the moment in which he had heard that Constance loved his rival, he became conscious that he had hitherto flattered himself with the persuasion that her heart was his own. When he had reached a part of the Forest considerably distant from the spot where he had left Lord Frederic, he threw himself heavily on the grass, and abandoned his soul to the desponding thoughts which the discourse he had heard suggested to him.

"Lord Frederic is then beloved by Constance!" said he to himself: "the modest maid, whose eyes were cast down if mine too fondly gazed upon her, has looked on him with tenderness! False, changeful Constance! Yet why do I accuse her? what right had I to her affection? what encouragement did she ever afford to my hopes? To the love which I never avowed to her, what return could I expect?—Ah! why did I quit her without declaring myself? What idea could she form of the strength of a passion, of which, even in her presence, I was sufficiently master to bury it in silence? During the years that have elapsed since I parted from her, perhaps she has never heard my name pronounced; and, if she has afforded it any place in her remembrance, she has perhaps thought of me as of one from whose heart the impression of her charms was already effaced; she has fancied herself more assured of the affection of the casual admirer who has told her she is fair, than of him to whom she is dearer than his life!—Ah! why did I quit her without declaring myself?"

Sir Albert continued to dwell on this idea with infinite anguish, and would gladly have given years of his future life to recall but a few of the moments which he had formerly passed in the presence of Constance, when, certain of her indifference to every other, his heart had secretly flattered him she was not without some prepossession in his favour, and when, had not his generosity forbidden him every attempt to improve that prepossession, he might possibly have gained the love, of which one whose black and murderous designs rendered him so unworthy of her, now boasted that he was the object. By degrees, as Sir Albert repeated to himself Lord Frederic's words, a faint hope arose in his breast, that the confidence with which that fierce youth had spoken of the favour of Constance, might have little other foundation than his own vanity; but the satisfaction which this idea afforded him, was almost instantly lost in the recollection, that, whatever might be the state of her affections, the Baron of Dornheim was within three days to receive her hand. He started from the ground, and stood for some moments almost bereft of thought and reason. A wish presently rushed upon his mind, to see her once more ere that fatal event for ever tore her from his hopes. He had not power to deny himself that last gratification; but determined immediately to seek admission to her presence, to tell her that his latest breath should wish her happiness; and then, bidding an eternal adieu, to his country, to join the armies of the Crusaders, and seek, amid the swords of the Infidels, that death which would then be the only object of his desires.

Animated by this design, he walked on; but he knew not which path would lead him to the Castle of Hertzwald, and in that wild Forest he had little chance of meeting with any one from whom he could obtain directions. He was provoked, to think that he might possibly have taken a road which would lead him a contrary way from that which he intended; yet he still walked on. At last he descried some turrets through the trees: but much was he disappointed, when, on a nearer approach, he knew them for those of Dornheim. He turned away with horror from the abode of his rivals, and struck into another path; in which fortunately he had not proceeded far, when he perceived a peasant before him. He hastened to over-take him, and inquired the road to the Castle of Hertzwald. The man was himself going part of the way thither, and offered to be his guide. As they walked together, the peasant asked Sir Albert many questions; but his answers were short, and often foreign to the purpose: yet, when his conductor demanded of him where he meant to lodge that night, it suddenly occurred to him, that, in the event of his not being so fortunate that day as to obtain an interview with the Lady Constance, it would be his wish to remain in the Forest till the next; and he asked the peasant whether he dwelt near, and would afford him a lodging in his cottage? The peasant replied, that he dwelt not far from the spot where they first had met; and readily agreed to give him such accommodation as he was able. They soon came within sight of the Castle of Hertzwald: Sir Albert parted from his guide, and proceeded towards it.

He knew but little of the Father of the Lady Constance, who, during the time of his former acquaintance with her, had been absent on a journey, and her Mother, with whom she had then resided at Prague, was since dead. He was hesitating what motive he should assign for his visit, when he observed a domestic at the gate: of him he asked some questions, and learned from his answers, that the Baron of Dornheim was at that time at the Castle, and was to dine there. This intelligence was sufficient to deter Sir Albert from seeking admittance till after his departure; for he felt that it would be impossible for him to command his emotions in the presence of his rival. He therefore quitted the gate, and determined to wait in the vicinity of the Castle till evening. He began to walk to and fro, often looking wistfully up at the windows, wishing he could know which were those of the apartment of Constance. He meant to keep at some distance from the walls; yet often some accidental shade on one of the casements was magnified by his imagination into an human figure; and he hastily approached, almost expecting he should find that it was the Lady Constance herself.

At last, the reflection that he might be observed by the domestics, and incur suspicion, induced him to quit the front of the Castle, and turn into a path which wound behind it. The Castle of Hertzwald was much inferior in size and strength to that of Dornheim: pleasure, rather than defence appeared to have been the object of its founder. A magnificent garden lay behind it, fenced from the Forest by a high wall, surrounded with battlements. Sir Albert walked on under this wall, with no other view than to pass away the time till the departure of his rival, whose happiness mean while, in enjoying the presence of the Lady Constance, distracted his soul with jealous pangs.—At an angle of the wall was erected a square turret, of which the windows looked out upon the Forest. Sir Albert was passing by it, when a voice caught his ear. He looked up; and a window being open, he could distinguish two female figures in the chamber within; but their faces were not turned towards him. With an involuntary curiosity he approached nearer; and could then hear, that she who spoke was endeavouring to comfort the other, who was weeping violently, and with many of the arguments so unavailing to those whose affliction is real, was urging her to restrain her tears.

"Suffer me to weep!" returned at last a gentle voice—it was the voice of Constance; and the heart of Sir Albert instantly acknowledged the sound.—"It was but to weep at liberty," pursued she, "that I so earnestly sued for permission to retire hither."

"You have never yet, Madam," rejoined the other, "so totally resigned yourself to grief as you do this day."

"This is perhaps the last time," replied Constance, "when I may be permitted to indulge my sorrows. Hitherto, indeed, they have been mitigated by a faint hope that I might be able to move my Father's heart, and to obtain at least a little longer respite from this dreaded marriage; but now that hope is lost!"

"But, if this marriage be indeed so hateful to you, Madam," said the other, "why will you submit to it?"

"Alas! Elinor," cried Constance, "how canst thou ask me such an idle question? Have I not already done all that maiden modesty would permit me, to avoid it? Have I left any means untried, to gain my Father from his purpose? Have not my unwearied supplications repeatedly awakened his fiercest anger, and provoked him to treat me with a harshness, which, but a few months since, I could not have supposed I should have survived? Thou knowest how little he regards my tears; and if to-day I have obtained this small indulgence to withdraw myself from the Baron's presence, I have owed it rather to the fear lest he should too plainly perceive, by my demeanour, my reluctance to the marriage, than to any pity for my sufferings: but the Baron does know my reluctance to the marriage. I one day collected sufficient boldness to avow it to him, in the hope, that, if his soul were capable of any generous feelings, he would of his own accord, reject the hand of a maiden whose heart was averse to him; but I soon found that I have judged too highly of him; and that the only effect of my avowal was, that he pressed the marriage with greater eagerness than before, lest delay should afford me time to devise some means of escaping it."

"And I still think, Madam," said Elinor, "that those means might be found. You are not watched— why should you not fly from the Castle?"

"And whither should I fly?" returned Constance. "Were any place of refuge open to me, thou may'st assure thyself I should be watched. What friend have I, in whose protection I could trust? In what Convent should I find a secure asylum, should the Baron of Dornheim require me to be given up?—Thou knowest how far his power extends.—And what dangers more dreaded than death might I not apprehend, should I, an helpless maiden, encounter singly the terrors of this wild Forest?"

"I must entreat you, Madam," said Elinor, "to forgive me for what I am about to say: the interest I feel in your concerns could alone urge me to a question, which I trust you will be too well assured of my attachment, to ascribe to impertinence or curiosity.— The Baron of Dornheim is not indeed a man who could ever have been very likely to gain your love; but yet, pardon me if I imagine, that, so submissive as you have ever hitherto been to the will of your Father, you would not, in this only instance, have expressed so much reluctance to obey him, had not your aversion to the alliance proposed, originated in some stronger motive than any personal dislike to your suitor. Though he is older than yourself, his person is still handsome and his air noble; his conversations I have heard yourself allow to be agreeable; of his character you have indeed reason to think unfavourably, since the instance you have mentioned of his ungenerous conduct; but you were equally anxious to avoid the marriage while he was only known to you by the report of your Father, who so earnestly sought to prepossess you in his favour.—May I then avow to you the suspicion which I have long entertained, that, had your affections not been otherwise engaged, the Baron of Dornheim would more easily have obtained your hand? And may I presume to solicit you to repose in me a confidence, of which you might be assured my fidelity were worthy, which would certainly greatly ease your mind, and might possibly enable me to render you some service?"—

Elinor paused—and the Lady Constance did not immediately return an answer.—At last, "If I had hitherto confined such a secret in my breast," said she, "were this a moment to declare it?"

"This were the only moment," returned Elinor; "another may not be allowed you!"

"Thou sayest true!" said Constance, bursting afresh into tears: "after to-morrow—Heavens! what a thought! —after to-morrow, it will be criminal to recollect that ever I have seen him!"—

"I have then judged rightly," cried Elinor; "but, Madam, since you have avowed thus far, may I not ask further, to whom it is that your affections are so deeply engaged?"

"And what would it avail me to tell thee?" returned Constance:—"I cannot!—my lips dare not pronounce his name."

"Will you permit me to name him, Madam?" said the Damsel.

"Thou canst not," cried Constance.

"And yet I have at times fancied I had discovered him," rejoined Elinor.

"Heavens!" exclaimed Constance, "and how have I then betrayed myself? What unguarded expression has ever escaped me?"

"Your lips, Madam," returned the Damsel, "have indeed never betrayed you; but of the language of your eyes you have been less conscious—when last Lord Frederic was here, you looked at him with an earnestness"—

"Is it possible I should have been observed?" cried Constance: "O! Elinor, durst I have spoken to Lord Frederic! Could I but have asked him one question!—I had once almost collected sufficient courage; but I met my Father's eye, and I dreaded lest I should inspire him with any suspicion. Methought, could I have spoken with Lord Frederic apart"—

Sir Albert listened, and the paleness of despair overspread his cheek.

"It would not be difficult to find an opportunity of speaking with Lord Frederic," said Elinor;—"many such"—

"Will occur in the castle of Dornheim," said Constance impatiently; "but it will then be too late.—I cannot, it is true, give my heart to the Baron; but never, when my hand shall be his, will I indulge it in any voluntary recollection of another—yet, could I but know he lived!"

"Who lived, Madam?" cried Elinor: "of whom are you speaking?"

"Didst thou observe the casque Lord Frederic wore that day?" said Constance.

"Of which the crest was a dragon with expanded wings?" demanded Elinor.

"I would I could know," said Constance, "how that casque came into his possession?"

"And in what manner could that interest you?" rejoined the Damsel.

Sir Albert listened more eagerly than before.

"If I mistake not greatly," returned the Lady Constance, "that casque had once another owner."

"To whom then did it belong, Madam?" said Elinor.

"To one whom thou hast never seen," replied Constance;—"to one whom I will never see again!"

"Was he then the Lover who gained your affections?" demanded the Damsel.

"He loved me once," said Constance, "but he knew not with what sentiments I regarded him. I was persuaded that my Father would never consent to our union; and I purposely slighted him, in the hope of eradicating from his breast a passion which could only render him miserable. It is now some years since I have seen him: and by this time he has questionless forgotten me. I hope he has;—for my destined marriage would become doubly afflicting to myself, if I thought that the news of it would give his heart a pang.—It is impossible but that he must have forgotten me—yet I have not forgotten him!"

"And how can you imagine it possible he can have forgotten you?" replied the enraptured Albert, presenting himself before the window.—"Ah! loveliest Constance! how little are you acquainted with the power of your own charms, if you suppose that the heart which once confessed it, could ever know a second love!"

At the sound of his well-known voice, Constance flew to the window; but when she beheld him, she trembled, and had nearly fainted; and, when she would have spoken to him, his name was all that she was able to pronounce.—He gazed on her with a transport which left him no remembrance of any of the difficulties which still remained to encounter.

"My adored Constance!" exclaimed he, "how infinitely am I repaid at this moment for all the sufferings of my tedious absence!—though banished from your presence, I have been insensible to every pleasure; though equally unconscious and undeserving of your love, every anxious fear, every jealous doubt has distracted my soul!"——

"But whence—" cried she, with an hastening and interrupted voice—"how came you—? In this remote Forest I had not expected—I thought you far distant:—what chance has brought you hither?"

"My impatience to review you," returned he, "was the sole motive of my journey. I could no longer support the anguish of my separation from you.—And at what a moment has my happy fortune led me to this Castle!—at the moment, lovely Constance! in which your lips have declared, that, unworthy as I am of any place in your remembrance, you have not forgotten me!"

"Heavens!" exclaimed she, "and have you then heard what I have carelessly spoken?"

"Can you forgive me, dearest Constance?" said Sir Albert: "I expected to have heard you avow your preference of my rival; the apprehension was too painful to be borne; and I could not resolve to tear myself from the spot where your voice first caught my ear, till the dreadful certainty should free me from the torture of suspence:—from that I indeed am freed; and the fear lest I should have incurred your displeasure by presuming to listen to your discourse, is now the only trouble of which my soul is insensible.—Can you forgive me, Constance?"

"If you have occasioned me any displeasure," returned she, "it has been by the suspicion which impelled you to listen. I would not, methinks, that you should have heard with what sentiments I thought of you;—but that you should suppose I harboured such for any other:"—

Overcome with joy at this unexpected meeting, Sir Albert spoke freely of the love which, for so many years, he had buried in unbroken silence; and the Lady Constance, forgetful of the reserve which had formerly induced her to reject even his most distant courtesies, acknowledged the affection with which he had long since inspired her heart. She was, however, the first who awoke from this dream of transport; she recollected her situation, and burst into tears.—He eagerly demanded their cause.

"Alas!" cried she, "we have only met, that we may the more severely feel the pain of our eternal separation!"

"Never!" exclaimed he; "never, my Constance! shalt thou be torn from me!"

"But how," said she, "can I escape the dreadful fate to which they destine me?"

"Fly from their power!" returned Sir Albert: "this arm shall shield you from pursuit!—It is not my own interest," pursued he, "which could ever have induced me to urge you to such a step. When I formerly knew you, encircled with prosperity, I would rather have died than have proposed to you to share my poorer fortunes; and had you but now given me reason to suppose you could be happy with my rival, believe me, my Constance! no distraction to which such an idea would have driven me, could ever have inspired me with any wish to disturb that happiness. But, situated as you are, it is to rescue you from misery, not to ensure to myself the highest earthly blessing, that I intreat you to fly with me from him who would so unworthily avail himself of your Father's power to force you to the marriage which you dread. I know the delicacy of your mind; and I know how unavailing the splendour of the situation to which the Baron of Dornheim could raise you, would be to constitute your felicity.—I can offer you no riches; nor would I, even at this moment, my adored Constance! ask your hand, could I any otherwise than by receiving it, be entitled to the character of your protector."

The Lady Constance listened, and her heart acknowledged the generosity of those sentiments, of which the former conduct of Sir Albert had left her no room to doubt the sincerity: yet she hesitated to comply. Never had she hitherto disobeyed her Father, unless it had been by the involuntary affection she entertained for him whose merits deserved her tenderest love, but whose situation, she well knew, would preclude him from any chance in his favour. And now, to fly the marriage enforced by his commands, and to give her hand in opposition to his will:—she was alarmed at the idea, and her strict sense of duty forbade her to consent. But Elinor, who had hitherto taken no part in the discourse, now interposed, and, in the strongest terms, supported the proposal of Sir Albert. She urged every excuse which the peculiar situation of the Lady Constance offered for her compliance; reminded her in how short a time her escape from the Baron would be impossible; and placed before her, in the most odious colours, every circumstance of the projected marriage, which she knew inspired her with the greatest dread. She even represented to her the guilt she would incur by falsely plighting her faith to him, while she was conscious of the impossibility of recalling her affections from their first and only object. Against these arguments, against the persuasions of Sir Albert, and the pleadings of her own heart in his favour, the Lady Constance was unable to defend herself;—she yielded to their force, and consented to entrust herself to the protection of her Lover. Transported at her compliance, he would have had her instantly throw herself from the window where she stood, which was not so high but that she might have done it without danger; for he was anxious to avail himself of the present moment, as well because he feared lest she should recede from her intentions, as because many circumstances might intervene to render her escape, at any future time, less easy. But Elinor earnestly dissuaded her from this: she said that many of the Baron's attendants were wandering in the Forest, awaiting the time of his departure; and she was urging many other difficulties, when Sir Albert himself recollected a circumstance which obliged him to give up the idea; he had left his horses at the Castle of Dornheim; and it was impossible for Constance to proceed so far on foot as to the nearest Town where others might be procured. He therefore concurred in the arrangement proposed by Elinor, who offered, when all the family should be retired to rest, to admit him into the garden, towards which looked the chamber of the Lady Constance, who, on seeing him, should let herself down from the window, and should be conveyed by him to his horse. Elinor entreated that she might be the companion of her flight; to which she, with much satisfaction, agreed. It afterwards, however, occurred to the damsel, that it would be better if Sir Albert had the key of the garden, and were to admit himself: since then she need not quit her mistress at the moment when her presence might be of so much avail to support her spirits, and confirm her resolution; she could not at that time go in quest of it, because it lay in the room in which the Baron of Dornheim was entertained; but, as soon as she should quit the Castle, she said she could easily possess herself of it; and she requested Sir Albert to tell her where he might be found by her, when she should bring it to him. He described the situation of the Cottage of the Peasant who had offered him a lodging: and there she promised he should see her soon after sun-set.

After a little further discourse between him and the Lady Constance, which they terminated by the interchange of the most solemn promises of affection and fidelity, the necessity of his hastening to recover his horses, or to procure others in their stead, obliged him to tear himself from her. Ere he departed, she drew a white plume from her hair, and threw it to him from the window.

"Wear this in your casque," said she: "I shall distinguish it by the light of the moon; and I shall fly, without apprehension of mistake, to the only protector in whom I would confide!"

Sir Albert kissed the plume, and placed it in his casque. "May I ever give you cause to continue that confidence in me, my beloved Constance!" cried he:—"And be assured that I shall value this pledge of your affection more highly than my life. Good Angels guard you till we meet again!—till we meet!—transporting thought!—to part no more!"

Even that idea did not enable Sir Albert to quit the window without pain; but Elinor repeatedly reminding him of the importance of the expedition, he at last complied with her instances, and bade the Lady Constance a final adieu.

It had been his intention to repair to the Cottage of the Peasant, and to procure some messenger whom he might thence dispatch to the castle of Dornheim (whither he had resolved he never would himself return), to order his Esquire to hasten to him immediately with his horses. He deemed it unnecessary to make any excuse to the Baron for his abrupt departure, since Lord Frederic, whose more immediate guest he had been, might well suppose that it was in consequence of their conference in the Forest; and he left it to him to place it in what light he should chuse, to his Father. His purpose, however, was anticipated; for he was not yet out of sight of the Castle of Hertzwald when Maurice met him. The Esquire expressed great joy to review his master; and recounted to him, that, on his not returning with Lord Frederic, he had been much troubled; and after waiting some time without being able to procure any intelligence of him, he had at last concluded he must be gone to visit the Lady Constance, whom he well knew his impatience to review; and that he had therefore taken that road in quest of him. Sir Albert commended his diligence, and imparted to him the happy result of the conference he had with her, and her promise to fly with him that night from her Father's Castle: he added, that it was his intention to carry her to Vienna; and, as soon as the rites of the Church should have rendered her indissolubly his, to demand the protection of the Emperor, whose former marks of favour left him no doubt of obtaining it, against any exertions which might be made by the Baron of Dornheim to force her from him; and he flattered himself that the intercession of so powerful a mediator might dispose her Father to an earlier reconciliation than could otherwise be reasonably expected.

While he was speaking he heard the trampling of horses; and he retired behind some trees to avoid them. It was the Baron and his troop, returning to the Castle of Dornheim.—Sir Albert felt a degree of satisfaction, that he had quitted that of Hertzwald without having had the time to see the Lady Constance. After they had passed, he walked on with Maurice; and enquiring of him for his horses, the Esquire replied, that he had left them at the Castle of Dornheim, not knowing his intention to return thither no more. Sir Albert ordered him to go immediately, and bring them to him at the peasant's cottage; whither he had hastened himself, imagining that, since the Baron was already departed, Elinor would speedily visit him with the key which was to admit him into the garden of Hertzwald.

His generous temper, never open to mistrust, induced him to place a full confidence in the interest she had expressed in her mistress's concerns. The assertion of Lord Frederic, that one of the damsels of the Lady Constance was in his pay, had not, in those moments of joy, recurred to his memory; nor, though it had, would Sir Albert ever have suspected that damsel to be Elinor. Yet Elinor had for some time been won by the gifts of Lord Frederic, to convey to him private intelligence of every confidence her mistress reposed in her. She had hitherto flattered him with the persuasion, that the Lady Constance slighted his Father on account of the preference she felt for himself; and it was with a view of leading her to an avowal of this, that she had begun the conference, which, contrary to her hopes, had drawn from her the confession of her love for Sir Albert. Disappointed by this, and still more by his sudden appearance, Elinor had only listened to the discourse which ensued between them, with a view of betraying their mutual interests to Lord Frederic; and, having formed a scheme which she was persuaded would be very acceptable to him, she possessed herself of the key, and set out, not for the Cottage where Sir Albert awaited her, but for the Castle of Dornheim. She was closely veiled, lest any of the domestics of the Baron should know that she belonged to the Lady Constance; and, as it had been her custom in former visits she had made there, she inquired for one whom she knew to be particularly attached to Lord Frederic, by whom she was immediately and privately conducted to his chamber.

On his return from following Sir Albert, he had found that his Father had gone to the Castle of Hertzwald, whither himself had received no invitation; and he had passed the day alone, freely indulging the wild distraction of his mind, and forming new schemes of violence.—At the entrance of Elinor, his countenance was brightened by a gleam of hope; and he eagerly asked her what news she brought him?

"Such, my Lord" returned she, "as I trust, when you shall have heard it all, you will deem deserving of some thanks: but the first circumstance I must impart to you, will be little welcome—you have a rival, hitherto unthought of."

"Who?—what rival?" exclaimed he.

"Let me first, my Lord," said the damsel, "request you to tell me whence you obtained the casque you wore when last you visited our Castle?"

"I had it from a Knight in the Imperial service," replied Lord Frederic: "he lent it to me once, when I was upon a sudden expedition: I liked it—it was lighter than my own;—and I gave him another in exchange for it.—But what of that casque?"

"Was that Knight named Albert, my Lord?" demanded Elinor.

"He was," returned Lord Frederic.

"Then know in him," said she, "the favoured lover of the Lady Constance."

Lord Frederic started from his seat in fury; he recollected the manner in which his conference with Sir Albert had terminated in the morning, and he wondered he had not before discovered what he was now so incensed to learn. His rage vented itself in many horrid imprecations; and scarcely could Elinor restrain him from going instantly in quest of the rival, on whom he thirsted to avenge himself.

"Were you more calm, my Lord," said she, "I could direct you to a surer vengeance than your sword can give you."

"What vengeance?" cried Lord Frederic: "tell me of vengeance, and I will listen to thee."

"This night," returned Elinor, "Sir Albert is to steal away the Lady Constance. I know not whether she would have consented to this measure, had not I persuaded her; but I overcame her scruples; and I have promised to admit him into the garden, where she is to meet him."

"Thou, Elinor!" exclaimed Lord Frederic: "is this the friendship thou didst promise me?"

"I shall leave that to your own decision, my Lord," replied she. "Here is the key of the garden-gate; and here is a white plume, which if you place in the front of your casque, Constance will fly to you as to Sir Albert, and you may bear her whither you will."

"My excellent Elinor!" cried he: "in this device I recognize thy genius. This will indeed avenge me on them both!"

"Nor is this all, my Lord," resumed the damsel—
"When once before, unsuspicious of this pre-
occupation of her heart, I would have counselled you
to propose to the Lady Constance a flight with you, to
avoid the marriage to which I knew she was averse,
you objected the detriment which might arise to your
own fortunes, from an action which would so greatly
irritate your Father."

"I care not for that now," exclaimed the impetuous youth: "I would sacrifice my fortunes, nay my
life, rather than miss this glorious opportunity."

"But you need endanger neither, my Lord," returned the damsel—"I have offered to attend the
Lady Constance in her flight; let me therefore return
the following morning to the Castle, and I will throw
the imputation on Sir Albert, with such circumstances as shall not only prevent any suspicion from
fastening on you, but shall determine both her Father
and your own to wreak on him the rage which the
wrong they will suppose him to have done them will
inspire. I am going to him now, to inform him, as
from his mistress, that she will fly with him to-
morrow night, instead of this: to-morrow night,
therefore, he will voluntarily throw himself into
their hands; and judge, my Lord, whether the Baron
of Dornheim, believing him the rival who has robbed
him of his bride, will prove a reluctant executioner of
the severest vengeance your fury could dictate to
your wishes."

However satisfactory Elinor had imagined the
plot she had thus treacherously laid, would prove to

Lord Frederic, his transports still exceeded her expectations. He promised her the most boundless rewards, and, as an earnest of them, presented her with a rich jewel he wore on his finger. She received it with much satisfaction, and gave him such further directions as she judged necessary, with regard to the conduct he must observe, the more effectually to deceive the Lady Constance. She then quitted him, and hastened to the Cottage, where Sir Albert had long waited in anxious expectation of her. When he saw her approach, he went hastily out to meet her, and demanded whether she had brought him the promised key?

"Alas! no, Sir!" returned she, with well-dissembled concern—"the Lady Constance has sent me the reluctant bearer of a message, which, I fear, will greatly disappoint you: it will be impossible for her this night to leave the Castle."

"Impossible!" exclaimed Sir Albert: "O Elinor! what cruel tidings dost thou bring me! Will Constance violate her promise?"

"Not willingly, valiant Sir!" replied the damsel; "nor indeed are you to consider this any other than a short delay of a measure in which her happiness is, if possible, more concerned than your own. To-morrow night you may assure yourself she will be yours."

"But why not to-night?" cried he.

"Sir," answered Elinor, "when, after the Baron's departure, I went in quest of the key, I found that it had been removed from its customary place, and the

Lady Constance soon learned, with great disquietude, that her Father was gone from home on some sudden business, and that, uncertain at what hour he might return, he had taken with him the key of the garden, meaning to re-admit himself that way, without obliging his family to watch for him."

"But if he has taken the key," cried Sir Albert impatiently, "why cannot I scale the wall?"

"Alas! Sir," replied she, "and do you not then consider the danger of his returning at the moment to surprize you? Should he meet with you in your flight with the Lady Constance, what but eternal ruin to your hopes could be the consequence? He would certainly attempt to force her from you; and, should you defend her, think what would be her sensations should her Father fall by your hand! Her mind is so deeply impressed with the idea, that I am confident, no arguments you could urge, would persuade her this night to venture;—but to-morrow no such dangers will threaten you; and to-morrow you may depend on her flying with you, to escape the tyranny of those who would force her to espouse the man whom she detests."

Sir Albert was by no means disposed to content himself with this delay of his hopes; but Elinor said so much, and with such an appearance of a sincere attachment to his interests, that he was at last obliged to submit, and to consent to wait till the following night. The damsel promised to revisit him in the morning, to bring him word whether he might safely attempt another conference with the Lady Constance during the course of the day, and likewise to arrange with him finally the mode of her escape. She then quitted him, and went back to the Castle of Hertzwald; when to her mistress, who had longed for her return, she accounted for the length of her absence, by feigning that Sir Albert had detained her with innumerable questions respecting all that had befallen the object of his love during their tedious separation. The deceived Constance was pleased at every instance of the tender interest he took in her concerns; yet, during the absence of Elinor, her resolution had begun to waver, and her apprehensions of the guilt she should contract, by a marriage contrary to the will of her Father, had almost determined her to stay, and suffer him to sacrifice her happiness for ever. But the crafty discourses of the damsel revived so strongly in her breast her horror for the Baron, and her love for the valiant Albert, that she was confirmed in her former intentions; and, with a kind of dread lest further reflection should finally oblige her to renounce them, she awaited the hour appointed for her flight.

She retired earlier than usual to her chamber; for her consciousness of her intended disobedience overwhelmed her in the presence of her Father, with all the confusion of guilt; and, unaccustomed to dissemble, she fancied that her every look betrayed the hidden purpose of her heart. Had he conversed with kindness, she would have found it impossible to command her feelings; but, with more than usual harshness, he reproved her for the aversion she expressed towards him whom it was his pleasure she should espouse, and exaggerated the passion with which her charms had inspired the Baron, in such terms as tended only to heighten the disgust with which she thought of him. She heard in silence; for she dared not trust herself to answer; but, when she left the room, the idea struck upon her mind, that she quitted it, not for a night, but perhaps for ever; and she burst into tears. In her own chamber she wept for some time without restraint; while Elinor was busied in preparing such things as it was expedient she should be provided with on her journey.

In the mean time the family retired to rest, and the hour approached, at which Sir Albert was to arrive. The heart of Constance palpitated with expectation, and her tears ceased to flow. Nor had she expected long, before she descried a figure in the garden; his arms, as he advanced, glittered to the moonbeam; and he was soon so near, that she distinguished the white feather in his casque. He came under her window; and Elinor, apprehensive lest her mistress should observe that his voice was not that of Sir Albert, hastily desired to him, in a whisper, not to speak, lest he should be heard by any one who might yet be stirring in the Castle. He comprehended her meaning, and made her a sign of obedience. For Constance, it had been unnecessary to enjoin her silence:—for the first time in her life, she was about to commit an action, of which she doubted the propriety; and on that action the whole of her future fate was to depend:—her emotion was so strong, that it hardly left her the power of speech; and she would even yet have receded from her purpose, and remained at the Castle, but Elinor reproached her irresolution, and represented it to her, that if she neglected the present moment, escape at any future one would be impossible. She had previously provided a ladder of ropes, and the trembling Constance descended from the window.

Ere she reached the ground, her transported lover caught her to his breast; she was offended at a boldness so new to her, and disengaged herself from his arms, in a manner sufficiently expressive of her displeasure. Apprehensive of too soon alarming her, he restrained his passion, and with a respectful air, led her towards the gate of the garden, where a confidential servant was waiting with two fleet horses. He vaulted on one, taking before him in his arms his lovely and unsuspecting prize: his servant, in the same manner, took charge of Elinor; and applying spurs to their horses, they sat out with the utmost speed.

Meantime the real Sir Albert, little imagining for what purpose his name and crest had been assumed, had sat for some time, after the damsel had left him, indulging his disappointment at the message she had treacherously brought him. Maurice was not yet returned with the horses: Sir Albert wished for his arrival, that he might have with him one to whom he could speak freely on the subject which occupied him; and at last, impatiently rising, he walked forth into the Forest, where for a while he strolled, disquieting himself with inventing new obstacles which might arise to prevent the accomplishment of his hopes on the morrow. The night was now set in, and its shades seemed to offer some relief to the trouble of Sir Albert; for they revived in his memory the reflections which had agitated his mind, when, at a similar hour, he had traversed that part of the Forest the preceding night; and when he recollected how invaluable he should then have thought the certainty which he now possessed, of the love of Constance, he was ashamed of having so far suffered the delay of the promise, which she still meant to fulfil, to prey upon his peace: he endeavoured to divest himself of every desponding fear, and earnestly recommended the object of his affections to the protection of every Saint and Holy Angel.

He then recollected, that, by wandering at so late an hour, he was detaining from rest the peasant to whose courtesy he was indebted for a lodging; but he had attended so little to his way, that he was at a loss to determine which path would lead him back to his cottage. He was still hesitating, when he descried, at some distance, a light, glimmering through the trees. He hastened towards it; but soon perceived that it was brighter than could proceed from a candle in a peasant's window. Still he advanced:—it seemed to recede before him. Surprized, and struck with some emotion of dread, he still followed it; when suddenly it sunk into the earth, and Sir Albert perceived that he was at the mouth of the *Cavern of Death.*

His dream, the strange accounts he had received at the Castle of Dornheim, and the determination he had formed to explore the mysteries of that dismal place, of which the various events of the day had suspended the remembrance, now rushed at once upon his mind; the disappointment which had prevented his quitting the Forest that night, now appeared to him the interposition of that destiny which had reserved him for the discovery of some dire secret; and he resolved immediately to attempt the adventure, to which the inward presages of his soul so strongly impelled him.

The night was not dusk; but, in that spot, the thick shadow of the trees diffused a gloom through which objects were scarce discernable; yet a few gleams of light were reflected by a narrow but rapid stream, which, having its source in the innermost part of the Cavern, forced its passage through the rocks, a little below the only entrance it presented to human feet. That entrance, for many years untrod, was half overgrown by briars, amid which screamed the birds of night. Sir Albert attempted to separate the branches; but the want of a light embarrassed him; and, but a few paces beyond the mouth of the Cavern, the darkness was total. He judged it necessary to return to the peasant's cottage to procure a torch: as he now knew in what part of the Forest he was, he found the way thither without difficulty.

At the door he was met by Maurice, who was arrived then with his horses, and who had wondered at his absence, knowing that it was already the hour at which he had appointed to repair to the Castle of Hertzwald. Sir Albert acquainted him with the alteration that had taken place in his schemes, and with his intention to enter immediately the *Cavern of Death*. Maurice heard him with visible consternation, and would have remonstrated; but Sir Albert interrupted him—

"Be satisfied," said he, "that I require not thee to follow me. Wert thou less superstitiously fearful, thy company on such an adventure, would to myself diminish the sensation of awe with which my mind is even painfully impressed; but, coward as thou art, thou couldst afford me no assistance. Remain here with my horses, and await my return.—If no evil befall me, thou shalt see me ere the morning dawn."

He then went into the cottage, and demanded a torch. When the peasant heard the purpose for which he required it, he expressed the same horror which was visible in the countenances of all in whose presence the *Cavern of Death* was named.

"Alas! valiant Sir!" cried he, "what desperate project have you formed? No human being has ever entered it, and returned to the regions of the living."

Sir Albert continued unshaken in his resolution.—The peasant reluctantly gave him a torch, and he returned alone to the mouth of the Cavern.

Though his soul was fortified with a courage which rose superior to every danger, yet his imagination was affected by the various terrific circumstances which attended the adventure he had undertaken; and if his ear caught the light flutter of the leaves, or

76

if the shadow of a branch, agitated by the wind, waved across his path, he started, and for an instant fancied it supernatural.

When he reached the Cavern, he again attempted to disentangle the briars which obstructed his entrance; but finding it difficult, he drew his sword, and with that soon opened himself a passage. The birds, which had long been accustomed to roost undisturbed among their branches, now roused, flew out in such numbers, that Sir Albert found it necessary to retire a few steps, lest, as they all made towards the light, the motion of their wings should extinguish his torch. When they were dispersed, he again advanced; and finding the passage now clear, he commended himself to the protection of his Tutelary Saint, and entered the Cavern. For a few paces he proceeded with his sword still drawn; but his path soon became so difficult, by reason of the large fragments of the broken rocks over which he was obliged to climb, that he found it necessary to sheath it, that he might be at liberty to assist himself with his hand; and indeed of no encounter with such enemies as it might avail against, had he, in that place, any apprehension.

As he advanced, the horrors of the Cavern seemed to deepen. The chill damp air froze the current of his blood: the silence was only broken, at distant intervals, by droppings from the roof, encrusted with half congealed vapours. At every step he trod more lightly; and if sometimes his foot slid upon a smooth and slippery stone, his heart, at the sound beat with a quicker motion. By degrees, he approached the bed of the subterraneous stream which he had observed issuing near the mouth of the Cavern; and the death-like stillness of the place was interrupted by the noise of its current, first, murmuring at a distance, then, as his path wound nearer to it, roaring with impetuous fury over the rough rocks which obstructed its course.

Sir Albert now found himself obliged to stoop, for the roof was too low to permit him to walk upright. He advanced, and it became still lower; but, after he had proceeded a few steps on his hands and knees, it suddenly widened, and he found himself in a spacious and lofty part of the Cavern; though neither of its extent nor height could he form any accurate judgment, for its bounds were lost in impenetrable darkness. In that thick and obscure air, his torch cast no light but on the hand which bore it. Only when he climbed the steep banks which overhung the stream, the white foam of its waters enabled him to trace its course, where it fell from a high rock in a broken cataract.

The deafening noise of the torrent filled the soul of Sir Albert with an unknown horror: he descended precipitately from the bank, and retreated to a rock, which seemed on one side the boundary of the Cavern; against which he leaned, while his imagination, unrelieved by any visible object, and wholly occupied in the recollection of his dream, was left at liberty to represent to him, now, the hideous phantom hovering in the dusky air, and now, the fleshless warrior, shunning his embrace, and waving high the fatal sword.

Sir Albert did not long give way to these visionary fears, but strove by reflection to recall the firmness, which, at no moment of real danger, ever had forsaken him. He was ashamed of his weakness; and, recollecting that no circumstance which could authorize it had as yet occurred, he withdrew his arm from the rock, and would have proceeded to explore further, when he felt himself suddenly drawn back;—his heart gave a fearful beat; he turned his head with perturbation, but saw nothing near him; he looked eagerly on all sides, and at last, concluding his own terrors had deceived him, he would again have advanced from that spot, when again he felt himself drawn back; and instantly a Form, to which even his fancy could assign no certain shape, flitted by him through a chasm in the rock, which the darkness had before prevented his observing, but which, when he approached it, opened to his view a long narrow passage, leading downwards with a steep descent, at the further extremity of which he descried a small red flame;—it resembled the dog-star, when he sets bloodily in a misty horizon.

Sir Albert now summoned all his resolution, and descended the path.—Hitherto, the ground on which he had trodden had been hard and rocky; but now, at every step his feet sunk into a loose dry sand. Guided by the flame, which grew larger and brighter as he advanced, he soon reached a small and nearly circular vault, entirely illuminated by its radiance; and beyond this no further path appeared.

In this spot, thus supernaturally pointed out to him, Sir Albert was persuaded he was to meet the conclusion of the adventure. He crossed himself, and implored the protection of the Holy Angels; then, fixing his eyes on the flame, which hung in the air considerably above his head, he observed that it darted downwards, in a spiral ray, on a spot where the sand rose in a little hillock: and he heard around him a faint sound, like the fluttering of distant pinions.—He regarded the hillock, and observed somewhat glittering beneath the surface: he stooped, and removing a little of the sand, discovered the blade of a sword; but what were his emotions, when he perceived that the hilt was grasped by the dry cold hand of a skeleton!

The words of the phantom who had visited him in his sleep, were instantly present to his remembrance; and he dropped kneeling on the earth.

"Yes, injured Spirit?" exclaimed he; "thou whom I know not by what name to address, but who hast questionless led me hither, and art now invisibly present to my invocation! I receive thy gift! and I swear to allow myself no rest, till the vengeance shall be completed, in which, though by what mysterious connexion as yet I comprehend not, thou hast taught me to believe my own destiny involved!"

As he uttered these words, with an awe which half checked his voice, he extended his hand to take the sword; and instantly at his touch, the bony fin-

gers which held it, unclosed themselves, and left it in
his grasp. At the same moment the flame, with a
vivid flash, disappeared; and a sudden whirlwind arising, extinguished the torch, and involved Sir Albert
in an eddy of the sand.

His soul, already worked up to the highest pitch
of horror, now fainted within him; and he sunk on
the ground, almost as lifeless as the ghastly form
which lay beside him. He continued for some time
devoid of all sensation; and, when his recollection
returned to him, as he unclosed his eyes in total
darkness, he felt that his hand was laid on that of the
skeleton.—He drew it back with hasty terror.—He
again made an effort to recover his fortitude; and, rising, he listened to the rushing of the torrent, and
hoped, by following that sound, to find the passage
between the rocks by which he had entered that re-
cess. But suddenly it was rendered visible to him by
a light which streamed through it from the outer part
of the Cavern. He approached, and perceived several
lights moving in different directions across the further entrance; and he imagined he heard the steps of
feet, and the clash of arms; when, in an instant, a cry
of horror, uttered by many united voices, assailed his
ear; and amid the inarticulate shrieks of some, he
could distinguish that others exclaimed, "blood! a
cataract of blood!"

The Cavern now shook from its foundations, and
the voices were at once lost in a crash, which seemed
as if the whole frame of Nature were violently rent
asunder. The sound was reverberated from the hol-

low sides of the Cavern in repeated echoes, which by degrees died away, and again no noise was heard, beside the rushing of the torrent.

The lights had disappeared, yet still a faint glimmering remained, which enabled Sir Albert to discern the passage. Still grasping the fatal Sword, he now reascended his former path, and, on issuing out into the open part of the Cavern, he perceived that the glimmering he had observed was that of a torch, which lay unextinguished on the ground. Rejoiced to recover a light, he took it up, and soon discovered that the violent noise he had heard, had been occasioned by the fall of a huge fragment of the rock, under which, on a further examination, he perceived the mangled bodies of two men, whom its enormous weight had crushed.—Struck with new horror, he was regarding these wretched victims, when he heard behind him a deep and agonizing groan.—He started!—and after some interval, it was repeated.—He turned, and looking round, he at last descried an armed figure, lying prostrate on the earth.—As he approached him, this unknown person groaned again.

"Who art thou?" cried Sir Albert, bending over to regard him; "and what purpose led thee hither?"

The stranger, at the sound of a human voice, half raised his head, and discovered to Sir Albert the features of the Baron of Dornheim!—Astonished, and scarcely crediting his eyes, he stood for a moment silent; while the Baron, on beholding him, shrunk aghast! and again turning his face to the earth, lifted up his arm, as if to shroud himself from the view of some terrific object.

"Whither wouldst thou drag me, avenging Spirit?" exclaimed he, with a faint and trembling voice.

Sir Albert, accosting him by his name, demanded to whom he addressed himself, and what had thus strangely agitated him; but to all his questions he returned such disordered answers, as induced the Knight to believe that distraction had seized him. At last the Baron, with a sudden start, again raised his head, and, leaning on his arm, regarded Sir Albert with a fixed horror.

"Why do you thus wildly gaze on me?" cried the Knight; "do you not know me?"

"Know thee!" exclaimed the Baron; "Ah! too well I know thee!—And that Sword!—The moment threatened by the Phantom is arrived, and already is my family extinguished on the earth!"

"My Lord!" said Sir Albert, "these words bear no common meaning; and circumstanced as I am, they concern me too nearly to suffer me to forbear insisting upon an explanation of them.—Rise! and prepare immediately to answer the demand which the events of this night sufficiently authorize me to make."

The Baron rose, as if awed by some power he durst not disobey; but presently starting with new affright—"Yon ghastly vision!" exclaimed he; "that crimson torrent!—Save me—hide me from the view!"

"These are the terrors of guilt, my Lord!" cried Sir Albert; "and vainly would you strive to escape the visions created by your own accusing conscience."

"Vainly indeed!" replied the Baron—"yet, if thou wouldst hear the dire disclosure I must make to thee, in pity lead me from this scene of horror!—here, I cannot!—it is impossible!—they haunt me—the Dæmons of Vengeance haunt me, and the unappeased Spirit of the Dead hovers around me, and urges them to seize their prey!"

Sir Albert saw, that in effect his mind was too much disordered to permit him to make any connected narration in that dreary place, which impressed with dismay the heart even of the innocent; and he led the way towards the mouth of the Cavern, while the Baron followed him with unsteady steps.

They were in the narrowest part of their passage, when the light of Sir Albert's torch was reflected by the gleam of armour; he looked, and beheld a man half hid in a cavity of the rock. On finding himself discovered, the stranger came forth trembling, and falling on his knees, petitioned for his life. The Knight demanded wherefore he had sought to conceal himself? He acknowledged that he was one of the vassals of the Baron of Dornheim, by whom he had been brought into the Cavern to assassinate Sir Albert.

"Is this true, my Lord?" said the Knight, looking sternly around.

"It is most true," replied the Baron—"such was indeed my purpose; but the Agents of an Invisible

World have interposed, and I have vainly striven to resist the decrees of fate."

Sir Albert ordered the man to rise and follow them; and soon emerging from the Cavern, though night still reigned profound amid the Forest, her shadows, to the eyes of those who had so long been buried in that region of subterranean darkness, appeared almost the refulgence of day.

At the earnest entreaty of the Baron, Sir Albert advanced some paces, till they had reached a spot, out of hearing of the sound of the murmuring current: there pausing—"And now, my Lord!" said he, "I will proceed no further, till you shall have fully explained to me, as I know you are well able to do, the mysteries which the recesses of yon Cave enfold. Why are you thus aghast when you behold this Sword? And who was the murdered Warrior in whose fleshless hand I have found it?"

"That murdered Warrior," replied the Baron, "was thy Father!"

Sir Albert started!

"And in me," continued the Baron, "thou viewest his murderer!"

Sir Albert's hair stood erect with horror, and his eyes sparkled with unutterable fury.

"Suspend thy vengeance till thou hast heard me further," resumed the Baron: "I feel that the hour of retribution is arrived, and a power more than mortal compels me to unfold the tale I tremble to pronounce."

"Rodolph, Baron of Dornheim, was thy Father. He was my Brother—my elder Brother; and from the Holy Land was he returning, to claim the inheritance which, at the death of our common parent, devolved of right to him, when I, covetous to possess it, met him in this Forest, with a band of ruffians devoted to my interest. He was alone; but, with his native valour, and with that Sword, which had often drank deeply of the blood of Infidels, he long defended himself against his assassins. At last, overpowered by numbers, he fell; and, in the convulsions of death, he so strongly grasped the hilt, that one of my men, unable to force it from him, was about to strike off the hand which held it, when I forbade him. To none of the brave Knights who had warred in Palestine was the Sword of Rodolph unknown; and, should it be found in my possession, or in that of any of my people, a discovery that he had perished by our hands might have ensued:—I therefore commanded them to forego the rich spoil, and to conceal it, with the body, in the innermost recesses of yon gloomy Cavern. A report of his death upon the journey was then circulated; and no suspicion of my concern in it arising in the minds of any, I succeeded to the vacant Barony, of which I have ever since, in the opinion of the world, been the undisturbed possessor. But the world has not known the secrets of my own guilty heart. Often, at the still and solemn hour of midnight, has the Spirit of my murdered Brother visited me; sometimes in silence pointing to his wounds, and waving his bloody Sword, sometimes threatening me with vengeance, in a voice, of which, even in the hours of apparent festivity, the sound has ever continued in my ears.—Of five former Sons whom I have lost, the untimely deaths were announced to me by this Phantom; but the great and final stroke which was to complete the measure of my punishment, and for ever cut off my family from the earth, he taught me to expect at the moment in which his Sword should pass into the possession of his own rightful heir.—With what terror have I awaited that moment, those only can know, who, like me, have known the guilt of blood:—from a faint hope to evade the menace, I have made repeated efforts to regain the Sword; but the fear lest I should expose my crime to detection, forbade me to employ for that purpose any but those who had been my former accomplices; they severally attempted it; but their courage proved unequal to encounter the horrors of the Cavern. Meanwhile, I had recourse to every means, to discover who was that heir to whom the Sword was destined. I could obtain no further information, than that Rodolph, ere he went to the Holy Land, had espoused a Lady at *Prague*, under a feigned name, lest my Father, who had destined him for another alliance, should be made acquainted with the marriage; but what afterwards became of that Lady, or whether she had borne him another Son, I could never learn, but continued in a state of the most painful uncertainty till yesternight, when, on your first entrance, I for a moment fancied you the visionary object of my nightly terrors:—Your name was repeated by my Son, and I strove to suppress my strong emotions; but still your resemblance to the noble Rodolph had filled my mind with dire forebodings, and your ring too certainly confirmed them, for well did I remember it in the possession of my Brother. This morning, your own narration explained to me every circumstance which could yet give rise to any doubts. From that moment, your death was determined; and already had I concerted the plan of your assassination, when with dismay I learned that you were gone to explore the recesses of the *Cavern of Death*. The moment which was to restore to you the Sword of your Father, seemed now at hand:—by one desperate effort could I only hope to avert the fate impending o'er my house;—and to that effort some supernatural impulse seemed to urge me on, and to overpower the dread, with which even the distant view of a place which I fancied conscious of my crime, had hitherto inspired me.—I armed as many of my vassals as I durst confide in, and at their head I entered the Cavern, hoping to find you, bewildered in its labyrinths, ere you should have seized the Sword on which my destiny depended. Animated by this idea, neither I, nor two of my accomplices in the murder of your Father, the only two who still survived, seemed to remember our former guilty dread, till we reached the spacious vault in which you found me. There the awful rush of the torrent struck upon our souls, and, in a moment, revived our terrors. We ascended its bank—we beheld the foaming cataract—to our eyes it seemed a cataract of blood!—those of my attendants whose consciences accused them of no former crimes, uttered a cry of dismay at the dire prodigy, and fled; but we, whose hand had been crimsoned with the blood of Rodolph, stood, riveted by horror to the spot—but we stood not long, before the fall of the impending rock overwhelmed my two companions, of whom one was Maurice, your Esquire, but my ancient vassal."

"Maurice!" exclaimed Sir Albert; "was he disloyal?"

"From the moment when I acquainted him with your birth," returned the Baron, "his fears concurred with his former attachment to me, and with the rewards I offered, to induce him to betray to me your every design. It was from him I learned your purpose of entering the Cavern."

The Baron was proceeding, when the trampling of horses interrupted him:—he paused; and Sir Albert, looking round, descried a troop of men, who, guided by the light he bore, were hastening towards him. On their nearer approach, it was discernible that four among them, who were on foot, bore a corpse, on a bier made of interwoven boughs. The Baron's mind misgave him; he eagerly questioned them, and, while they hesitated to answer, he forced a passage through them, and rushed to meet the corpse; he recognized the pale and blood-stained features of his Son.

The bearers sat down their load.—The Baron uttered not a word, but threw himself on the bier, and in convulsive sobs, gave vent to the passions which agonized his soul.—Sir Albert drew near, and with

strong emotions beheld the face of Lord Frederic.—
The Baron suddenly turned, and before he was aware
of his purpose, snatched from his hand the Sword of
Rodolph, and plunging it in his own breast, sunk ex-
piring on the body of his Son.—The horsemen
alighted, and crowded round him; but succour was
too late;—pointing to Sir Albert, in a faultering ac-
cent he bade them regard in him their rightful Lord;
and then, drawing forth the weapon from the wound,
his life issued with it, in a stream of blood.

Sir Albert, falling on his knees, awfully adored
the severe justice of the Almighty Avenger of the
crimes of mortals.

Those who surrounded the bier, all vassals of the
Barony of Dornheim, were struck with consternation
at the fatal catastrophe, and eagerly enquired of each
other the meaning of their late master's dying words.
Sir Albert, in succinct terms, and without expatiating
on the guilt of him who lay lifeless before them, acquainted them with the discoveries which that night
had brought forth; a narration confirmed by him who
had been found concealed in the Cavern, and who
had been present at the Baron's confession; and all
most readily acknowledged the Son of Rodolph as
their Lord, and entreated him to suffer them immediately to conduct him to the Castle. He complied with
their request, and proceeded thither with them;
whilst those who had before borne the body of Lord
Frederic, now bore that of his Father with it on the
same bier.

On their way, Sir Albert demanded the particulars of the death of the former.—They confessed, that the Baron had sent them with orders to lye in wait for Sir Albert himself; but that the similarity of the arms and vestments of Lord Frederic had deceived them, and assaulting him, they had not discovered their mistake till he had fallen beneath their swords.

When they reached the Castle, where the chief officers and most of the domestics were in waiting to re-admit their Lord, the tidings they brought of his death at first diffused a general dismay; but Sir Albert convened the vassals in the great hall, and, in a modest, but forcible address, stated to them his claim to the succession, and adduced such proofs as left them no room to question his right to the domains of his Ancestors. Many of the older men who were present, remembered Lord Rodolph, and loved his memory; and they, with acclamations of joy, retraced his features in those of his Son; and, as the character of the late Baron had not been such as to engage the affections of any of his people, there were none who did not receive their new Lord with demonstrations of unfeigned gladness.

Sir Albert now wished to be alone, that he might reflect at leisure on the extraordinary events of the night, and compose the agitation of spirits into which so many unexpected discoveries had thrown him. But, as he was proceeding along a passage, in his way to a private apartment, the Seneschal followed him, and demanded what he would have done with regard to two Ladies who had been brought that night to

Castle, by the order of the late Baron. Sir Albert demanded who they were: the Seneschal unlocked the door of an apartment on one side of the passage, and Sir Albert beheld the Lady Constance! Surprized and delighted, he flew towards her; but her astonishment and joy seemed even to exceed his own.

"By what miracle art thou preserved?" cried she: "What Guardian Power has delivered thee from the foes by whom, when they tore me from thee, I left thee encircled?"

Her words seemed at first mysterious to Sir Albert; but Elinor, finding it impossible to avoid the discovery of her treason, threw herself at their feet, and voluntarily confessed it; and it then appeared, that after the Lady Constance, deceived by her arts, had betrayed herself into the power of Lord Frederic, she was still unconscious of her mistake, when they were assaulted by the troop which the Baron, informed by the similar treachery of Maurice of her intended flight with Sir Albert, had sent out to intercept them: that Lord Frederic had been obliged to set her down, in order to defend himself; and that two of the troop, in compliance with the orders they had received, had immediately seized herself and Elinor, and had borne them to the Castle, which they had reached about an hour before; during which interval she had abandoned herself to the bitterest grief, and had incessantly wept the inevitable death of the imaginary Sir Albert.

These circumstances afforded the pious Knight new cause to admire the dispensations of Providence, which had thus rendered the meditated crimes of the victims of its justice the means of bringing down its judgments on their heads; and he could not but feel some satisfaction, that his enemies had thus been the instruments of their own destruction; since he was now spared the task of avenging his murdered Father on one so nearly allied to him as the Baron, and of disputing his claim to the succession, with one with whom he had lived on such habits of intimacy as with Lord Frederic, till the impious proposal he had made him in the Forest had discovered to him the blackness of his soul. The Lady Constance heard with transport, of the change which that night had effected in the fortunes of her Lover.

The morning now began to dawn; and Sir Albert immediately dispatched a messenger to her Father, to inform him of the death of the late Baron, and his own succession, in right of his Father, Lord Rodolph—to acquaint him that his Daughter was at the Castle; and to invite him thither, to learn such further particulars as it was expedient he should know.

The invitation was immediately complied with; nor was Sir Albert deceived in his hope, that he who had been about, from motives of interest, to sacrifice his only child to a man so unworthy to possess her, would, with equal readiness, consent to bestow her on himself, who now enjoyed the power and dignities of his late rival. His proposals were received with manifest joy; and, till the marriage could be celebrated with proper magnificence, the Lady Constance returned with her Father to the Castle of Hertzwald, where, during that interval, Sir Albert, now universally acknowledged Baron of Dornheim, daily visited her.

He caused the bodies of the late usurper and his son to be privately interred; but the remains of his unhappy Father, himself, at the head of a large body of his vassals, re-entered the *Cavern of Death* to bring forth; and mourning his untimely fate with the deepest expressions of filial sorrow, he caused them to be deposited, with the most solemn rites of the Church, and every funeral honour, in the Chapel of the Castle; erecting over them a magnificent tomb, above which was suspended the fatal Sword.

Shortly after, he espoused the Lady Constance; and in the hand of her who had been the object of his earliest affections, he received the completion of that felicity to which his virtues entitled him.

FINIS.

NOTES

Page

15 **the Black Forest**: The Black Forest of southwestern Germany provided the setting for another Gothic novel published in 1794, Karl Friedrich Kahlert's *The Necromancer: or, The Tale of the Black Forest*. Forests had become popular settings for Gothic stories ever since Ann Radcliffe's 1791 *The Romance of the Forest*, and the dark, Germanic, forested backdrop of *The Cavern of Death* reappeared in numerous Gothic works in the ensuing decades.

18 **Frederick Barbarossa**: Frederick Barbarossa (c. 1123-1190) was the German King and Holy Roman Emperor from 1152 until he drowned during the Third Crusade in 1190.

19 **"I will not indulge these thoughts"**: The barriers of class and title that prevent Sir Albert from marrying Constance can be found at the heart of most early Gothic novels as well as most sentimental fictions of the latter eighteenth century. Novelists reflected shifting attitudes towards marriage as the companionate marriage began to gain favor over marriage for political and economic alliance.

21 **Meteor**: In this context, a meteor is a "luminous atmospheric phenomena" (OED).

21 **"He talked wildly of a Spirit who pursued him"**: The servants in Horace Walpole's *Castle of Otranto* (1765) also panic and act foolishly when confronted with seemingly supernatural events. Ann Radcliffe and Matthew Lewis continue this tradition in the 1790s.

22 **Seneschal**: "An official in the household of a sovereign or great noble, to whom the administration of justice and entire control of domestic arrangements were entrusted. In wider use: a steward, 'major-domo'" (OED).

23 **casque**: helmet

28 **brilliants**: fine diamonds

33 **Bohemian**: from Bohemia, what is now the western part of the Czech Republic.

34 **"assumed the Cross"**: One who has "assumed the cross" has sewn a cross on his tunic and declared himself a soldier of Christ in the Crusades.

34 **Baldwin the Second of Jerusalem**: Baldwin II was crowned King of Jerusalem in 1118. He was held hostage by the Turks from 1123-1124.

34 **Emir Balac**: Balak, Emir of Aleppo (Syria), captured Baldwin in 1123, but died a month before Baldwin's release in 1124.

40 **"whenever one male should be the only survivor of it"**: Another borrowing from Walpole's *Castle of Otranto,* in which Manfred's rule of Otranto is threatened by a vague, yet menacing prophecy.

79 **dog-star**: "The star Sirius, in the constellation of the Greater Dog, the brightest of the fixed stars" (OED).

82 **"two men, whom its enormous weight had crushed"**: Walpole's *The Castle of Otranto* begins with the "bleeding mangled remains" of young Conrad crushed beneath a giant helmet. Such gruesome scenes can be found in numerous Gothic works of the period.

93 **"Providence bringing down its judgments on their heads"**: Clara Reeve's *The Old English Baron* (1777) ends with a similar moral. Reeve states that the novel's events "furnish a striking lesson to posterity, of the over-ruling hand of Providence, and the certainty of RETRIBUTION."

Lightning Source UK Ltd.
Milton Keynes UK
UKOW04f1112040118
315542UK00001B/3/P